WOOED *by a* *Wicked* DUKE

Seductive Scoundrels, Book Five

COLLETTE CAMERON

Blue Rose Romance®
Portland, Oregon

Sweet-to-Spicy Timeless Romance®

WOOED BY A WICKED DUKE
Seductive Scoundrels

Cover Design by Kim Killion

Attn: Permissions Coordinator
Blue Rose Romance®
8420 N Ivanhoe St. #83054
Portland, Oregon 97203

eBook ISBN: 9781954307605
Paperback ISBN: 9781954307612

www.collettecameron.com

“And I make you nervous?”

His voice came out a silky purr,

and her tummy turned over.

He knew he did. *Wretched man.*

would, and she couldn't claim remorse for the deficit.

Her dratted expressive eyes gave away her every thought. She might as well blab them aloud, so transparent was she. Or so her sister, now the Duchess of Sutcliffe, claimed. In point of fact, Jessica wasn't altogether positive she'd be better off if she'd been able to master such a facade anyway. Plainly put, she wasn't deceptive by nature.

Her gloved hands wrapped about her shoulders to help ward off the sharp chill, she hurried forward rather than return to the crowded ballroom, with its abundance of sweaty bodies, cloying perfumes, and stifling atmosphere.

Stealing a few calming minutes outdoors, gathering her equanimity, and reining in her seething temper wouldn't result in a chill or ague. Possessed of a robust constitution, she rarely suffered from illness.

Wrestling her anger into submission might take more than a few minutes, truth to tell. Much more, such restrained fury simmered behind her ribs. No, she mightn't be dishonest by nature, but she did have a temper when incited. And, by damn, she'd just been provoked mightily.

Guilt poked her for silently swearing. Her parents would be mortified. Jessica gave a mental shrug. Sometimes an expletive was required, if only in one's thoughts, and despite being swathed in virginal hues.

Even with the mansion's windows aglow, her pale gown—unfortunately similar in color and style to those worn by every other insipid debutant present tonight—stood out in stark reprieve against the night's crisp darkness.

An image of dressed-up dolls on display came to mind—ladies on the Marriage Mart. Paraded before potential husbands, the misses' qualifications—or lack thereof, in her case—were easily attainable with a murmured request in the right ear.

She'd have preferred a rich emerald or royal purple gown, but young women were expected to appear pure and untouched in their shades of whites and ivories. Innocent. Unspoiled. Untouched. *Bah. What poppyswallop and baldercock.*

Or was it poppydash and balderswallop?

Jessica shrugged. What difference did it make?

What *did* matter—a great deal, truth be told—was that she mustn't do anything untoward to draw the acrid eye of an Almack's peeress or other noble.

Such as slap the faces of tart-mouthed, mean-spirited chits. No matter that they heartily deserved a harsh, public reprimand.

To do so would've brought immense satisfaction. Oh, indeed, it would've done. She tightly pursed her lips. Alas, immense censure, too. Disapproval, she could ill afford, more's the pity. Not that she'd give a hen's tail feather about what anyone thought about her.

Well, she might care a *little*, but not enough to change who she was. Such artifice sickened her. A grimace pulled her mouth downward.

Still, Jessica had promised to *try* to conform. She wanted to embody the epitome of decorum. To display pretty manners and modesty. Truly, she did.

Liar!

Fine…not truly. But she did strive to—to the degree she wouldn't knowingly disgrace herself or her family—and she still might also enjoy a lovely time. For London did offer ever so many entertainments and distractions. One Season ought to see her curiosity satisfied. Then back to the country for her, where she could be herself again. Where she wouldn't have to worry about every word or action.

Briskly rubbing her arms, Jessica wet her lower lip. As nippy as the outdoors was, she'd welcome a glass of lemonade or ratafia. She'd become quite parched while dancing in the ballroom's sweltering heat.

Her partners thus far had been amicable, the dancing passably good. She wasn't a nymph on her feet, so she didn't hold her partner to a higher standard than herself.

In fact, unable to locate her sister, brother-in-law, or a friend to accompany her, she'd decided—perhaps unwisely, she grudgingly admitted to herself—to make her way to the refreshment tables in search of a much-needed glass of…anything.

That was another silly rule. Why a young woman couldn't traverse a room milling with people without a chaperone did not make sense.

A most unpleasant encounter with a trio of claws-bared females had detoured her from her goal, and now her thirst remained unquenched. Three smugly satisfied female faces paraded before her mind. God save the poor chaps who ended up married to those mean-spirited shrews.

Prior to that, she'd genuinely been having a grand time, her youthful bashfulness no longer a constant, exasperating presence. Why, her dance card bore the names of several gentlemen—including no fewer than three dukes. And although undoubtedly not the belle of the ball, she couldn't complain that her first official foray into Polite Society was a dismal failure.

She permitted the tiniest little proud smile to arc her mouth. It seems she truly had outgrown her shyness. Not that she'd ever be outgoing or seek attention. A diamond of the first water she was not, nor did she have any desire to be. Not that she was a dowd, by any means.

Though appropriately white, her gown, with its delicately embroidered overskirt and seed pearls, was a confection straight from a fairytale, as was her sapphire parure and her intricately styled hair.

Theadosia, her dearest sister, vowed the sapphires exactly matched Jessica's eyes. Not exactly. Her eyes were green-blue. Nonetheless, she quite felt like a princess, silly as that might seem.

As a little girl, she'd always pretended she was a princess. Only, as an innocent child, she'd believed a charming prince would fall madly in love with her. Never mind she was a humble vicar's dowerless, youngest daughter.

Not dowerless any longer.

She shoved the intrusive thought aside and resumed her fanciful reverie. Dowerless worked better for her daydream, and fairytales weren't based in reality, after all. It was much more romantic to wed for love than to be bartered off for a substantial marriage settlement, a title, or a parcel of land.

Her handsome and oh-so-entrancing prince would place her before him on his magnificent white steed—for fairytale princes must always ride white steeds—and they'd gallop away into the burnished sunset to live happily, passionately ever after. Because, quite naturally, happily-ever-afters required passion.

A wry smile tilted the edges of her mouth.

Twaddle, rubbish, stuff and nonsense. The whole of it.

Jessica had been all of ten when she first realized marriage was often something far different than happily-ever-afters. Nevertheless, good fortune did fall upon a lucky few, like her older sister, Theadosia, and her adoring husband, Victor.

They boasted friendships with several prominent peers and could be credited with her pleasant reception and acceptance into *le bon ton* so far. Almost everyone she'd met had been agreeable, if a trifle stuffy, formal, and exuding self-import.

But the upper ten thousand held pompous, elevated opinions of themselves and believed everyone else ought to as well. They also hid their true characters behind facades. At least, that was her perception of them thus far. Most were harmless, but a few—like the viper-tongued Medusas she'd just overheard—were the embodiment of cruelty and spite.

Vicious gossips.

She couldn't abide tattlemongers in any form.

People who had nothing better to do than spread rumors as casually as buttering warm toast. Or who were such miserable wretches they sought to make themselves feel better by disparaging others. The worst of the chinwag lot, however, were those that contrived *on dit* simply because they enjoyed the trouble their tarradiddles wrought.

Such were despicable, contemptible dolts, and she had no patience for them or their nastiness. Nor did she have any desire to be their target, which meant she'd need to return to the ballroom before her next dance.

Pulling her eyebrows together, she studied the elaborate fan-shaped dance card.

If she recalled correctly, this set remained unclaimed. She'd be remiss to leave a partner searching for her. Such inconsideration wouldn't do. Not when she must remain above reproach. Already, dishonor hovered about her family like a soiled gray mantle.

Initially, she'd been eager to leave Colechester behind, mistakenly believing the mortifying shame and humiliation of Papa's disgrace would lessen with a bit of distance between her and the parish he'd stolen from. How wrong she'd been.

It was almost as if *le beau monde* was waiting, watching, expecting her family to misstep, and if they inadvertently did, those lofty denizens would pounce like a panther on a defenseless gazelle.

After perusing the dance card in the filtered light, Jessica relaxed a fraction.

Yes, she was free for the next thirty minutes. However, the dance afterward was promised to Crispin Rolston, the enigmatic Duke of Bainbridge. The arresting nobleman had positively flummoxed her by explicitly requesting that particular waltz.

She scrunched her forehead further, uncertain why a degree of unease coiled in her belly, making her shudder in apprehension.

Bainbridge was a pleasant enough chap. Quite dashing, actually, if she were wholly honest. *Oh, very well.* Extremely dashing. From the moment she'd laid eyes upon him, she thought so. She'd encountered him several times in the past year, and he'd grown impossibly more stunning upon each occurrence.

Why had God deemed the male of the species should be the more attractive? It was most unfair. As a young girl of perhaps eleven or twelve, she'd voiced that thought to her mother. Mama had laughed and said that was often true of birds but not necessarily of humans and other animals.

The Duke of Bainbridge made her sweet, pious mother into a liar.

His rakish smile could melt a glacier. And those eyes. *Lord, those magnificent eyes.* Quicksilver gray, they shone with a seductive gleam that had stolen her breath more than once.

Not, by Jove, that she'd ever admit such a thing. Vicar's daughters didn't entertain such notions. *Seductive gleam? Stolen breath?* She shook her head in self-reproach but allowed her mind to wander a bit longer.

Bainbridge's wavy, dark-blond hair—a lovely shade similar to sugared pecans—had a tendency to fall over his noble brow, enhancing his devil-may-care roguishness. His sculpted cheeks, angular jaw and chin, striking, almost severe eyebrows—several shades darker than his hair—and the sharp blade of his nose all added to his masculine appeal.

He was tall, of course, but not overly so. She didn't have to crane her neck to meet his startling eyes. And he had nice hands: clean nails, square tips, a light smattering of honey-colored hair across the knuckles.

Couldn't he have one flaw? Crooked teeth? Long nostril hair? Bad breath? A squeaky voice?

Honestly, she was hard put to find a single fault in his appearance. Neither, evidently, could the dozens of other simpering, ogling women continually surrounding him. To Jessica's credit, she didn't blink like a fly had landed in her eye, turn lobster red, or trip over her tongue in his presence. He was, after all, just a flesh-and-blood man.

Yes, but such a scrumptiously attractive one.

If she could've scolded her subconscious for stating the obvious, she would've done so.

But it was his voice, such a deep, resonant timbre, she found nearly irresistible. Jessica could listen to him speak for hours. Did he sing? She thought he might with that voice—as rich as melted chocolate. She'd never sat close enough to hear him when the hymns were sung the few times he'd attended Sunday services.

Placing her palms flat on the balustrade, she breathed out an exaggerated sigh. Crispin, Duke of Bainbridge, in all his sleek, male glory, was precisely the stuff of which fairytale heroes were made.

No. He isn't!

She narrowed her gaze at his name, scrawled across her dance card in penmanship as indolent as the scoundrel himself. Bainbridge was exactly the type of wicked libertine and philanderer Papa had always warned his daughters against.

Handsome. Wealthy. Confident. Privileged. Charming.

Rakehell. Roué. A man about town. Heartbreaker. Scoundrel.

Papa's list of unfavorable characteristics went on considerably longer. Pages longer. And yet, her own father, a clergyman, couldn't cast stones. Not with the burden of his own sins made so very public. In truth, the duke was the more honest of the men. He didn't hide his flaws behind piety.

Bainbridge was an aristocrat who drew women of every station and status to him like plump, fragrant summer blossoms enticed, clumsy, nectar-drunk bees. If his allure weren't so awfully pathetic to witness, she might find female reactions to him amusing.

Elderly dames batted their stubby eyelashes while thrusting out their saggy bosoms, hoping for a kind word or one of his devastating smiles. Married women and widows curved their painted mouths upward seductively and slid him inviting glances.

Precisely what those invitations entailed, Jessica refused to ponder, lest her cheeks heat with blistering color. Blushing debutantes and calf-eyed wallflowers observed his every move with something akin to hunger—or huntresses stalking their unsuspecting prey.

Albeit, he couldn't precisely be stalked when he knew full well—exploited, even—the enticing effects he had on women.

Extraordinarily, as much as she could appreciate his attractive outward trappings—she did have perfectly good vision, after all—Jessica had never been physically attracted to him.

Except for the difficulty in breathing on occasion. And my irregular pulse that one time.

She pressed her lips tight. *Fine. Thrice.*

And then there was the time your tummy went all wobbly, her annoying conscience gleefully reminded her.

Bah! She'd made it a point never to let her guard down around Bainbridge. To do so was utter idiocy. He was a seducer of innocents. A hedonist. A man with a new mistress or lover every month.

Or so she'd heard whispered. Not always in shocked disapproval, either. No, often there'd been yearning, possibly even a morsel of admiration, in those covert discussions.

While Jessica might have a tendency toward shyness and was by no measure a woman of the world, she assuredly was not an empty-minded fool, either.

She wasn't worried about standing up with him, however. On the once beautifully chalked dance floor, in full view of all, he'd be required to act the gentleman. Point of fact, she'd never known him to do otherwise with her, despite his reputation as a debauchee.

A particular friend of her brother-in-law, Bainbridge wasn't bacon-brained enough to attempt anything untoward and risk Victor's wrath. In any event, he'd never shown the least interest in her.

Of course, Jessica had spoken to the duke previously, just the two of them. Several times, in truth. Had, in fact, bested him at a game of Pall Mall a few weeks ago. Why come to think of it, he still owed her an ice from Gunter's as her prize.

Oh, he'd better not think to renege, the cad.

She meant to collect on that ice. Or a sorbet. *Mmm.* She shut her eyes for a blink, imaging the deliciousness melting on her tongue. Sorbets were even more scrumptious than ices, particularly the lemon-flavored frozen treat.

She adored almost anything flavored with lemon. Lemon curd, lemon drops, and lemonade amongst her other favorites.

Upon reflection, she concluded Bainbridge had

probably only signed his name to her dance card as a favor to Victor. But of course. That made the most sense. She suspected as much of a few of the other gentlemen who'd also requested dances.

Not that she minded.

Far better to be partnered out of obligation than to lurk with the sad-eyed wallflowers gazing wistfully, sometimes sullenly and enviously, at the other misses enjoying themselves. In truth, she'd expected to be amongst the wallflower ranks, but she should've known Theadosia and Victor would assure she was not.

They, and the Duchess of Pennington—the sister of her bosom friend, Ophelia Breckensole—would never permit her to pine away as an onlooker at the ball. Ophelia's twin, Gabriella, the new Duchess of Pennington, no doubt played a not-so-subtle part in encouraging gentleman to seek a dance with Jessica as well.

She didn't mind their interference since affection motivated them. They were dears, one and all. Ophelia would be wondering where she'd disappeared to, though. Jessica shouldn't linger too much longer.

As she made her way to a secluded corner and leaned against a balustrade overlooking a quaint, walled garden alit with lanterns, beyond which lay what must be a hothouse, she pressed her mouth into a prim line and permitted her shoulders to slump. Slivers of iridescent moonlight bathed the garden and a figure-eight-shaped pond in a shimmering, silvery glow. The picturesque scene almost appeared fairylike.

Snorting, she shook her head and rolled her eyes heavenward. There she went again with her fairytales. She was much too old to harbor such nonsensical fancies.

A toad's throaty croak echoed from the vicinity of the foliage edging one side of the pond. Its raspy calls reminded her of the humble parsonage in Colechester where she'd spent her girlhood. A wave of homesickness and an intense longing to see her parents engulfed her.

It would be at least a year, likely two or three, before she saw them again. At times, she felt such a burden to Victor and Theadosia. She'd been foisted upon them as newlyweds. They never complained, but Jessica felt she was an imposition.

A shiver scuttled up her spine, and she renewed rubbing her arms.

How very different her life had been less than a year ago.

Before scandal had sent her disgraced father to an Australian penal colony to minister to criminals. How stupid and naïve she'd been to believe the *on dit* wouldn't follow the Brentwoods from Colechester to London.

A well-respected solicitor, her brother, James, didn't give a fig what Society thought. Her eldest sister, Althea, had eloped several years ago and was happy as a grig with her husband and children. And, of course, Theadosia had made a love match with Victor, the Duke of Sutcliffe.

No one looked askance at the Sutcliffes and didn't reap the consequences.

Jessica, alone, had the most to lose from the ugly murmurings—namely, a respectable match. But she wasn't altogether keen on landing a husband, unless she loved him. Her mother's and sisters' marriages had given her high expectations. Perhaps, unrealistic expectations. *Fairytale* expectations.

But why shouldn't she desire love? Wait for love?

Without love, how did one forgive? Find contentment and happiness? Bear the heartaches and difficulties life served up more often than not? With a loving spouse, someone to support and encourage, a man she could trust her deepest secrets and innermost desires to, she could be more than satisfied.

Even when Mama had railed at Papa because of the shame he'd brought upon the family, she'd never stopped loving him. She'd willingly accompanied him to Australia, leaving her grown children behind. Leaving Jessica with Theadosia. Because a single woman, even accompanied by her mother and vicar father, had no place amongst hardened convicts.

With deliberate intent, she inhaled a deep, cleansing breath of chilly air. As she exhaled, she released her concerns. It was too early in the Season to be mooning about such piffle.

If she didn't meet a man who looked at her the way Victor regarded Theadosia, or the Duke of

Pennington gazed at Gabriella, the world wouldn't tilt on its axis, nor would the sun fail to rise.

At almost twenty, she wasn't quite on the shelf or in her dotage. There was yet time. Not all would agree with her assessment. *Breeding years and all that claptwaddle.*

Inhaling the cleansing air again—it was most invigorating—she deliberately tried to turn her thoughts to more pleasant musings. A Come Out and a Season had never crossed her mind, even after Theadosia married Victor. He'd generously dowered her, too.

Now, here she was. In London. At a posh ball. With a new wardrobe, a sizable settlement, and about to launch into her first Season. Not the merest bit terrified.

Really?

Fine, perhaps a trifle nervous.

The breeze toyed tauntingly with the curls on either side of her face.

Uh-hum, mocked that perturbing voice that never permitted her to lie to herself.

Very well. She was entirely out of her element but

determined to do her best. For Theadosia's benefit. And Victor's. And, yes, even for James's sake, too.

Damned, dashed nuisance to have such a rational conscience.

She *had* been having an enjoyable time earlier. Much better than she'd anticipated, until she'd overheard that trio of sharp-clawed she-cats gossiping about her and Theadosia. Or, more on point, about Papa's public dishonor.

Positive they'd seen her approaching the refreshment tables, in *sotto voce* voices, they'd tittered and feigned shock about his embezzlement of church funds and the subsequent gambling away of said monies. Of nearly finding himself defrocked. Of Theadosia almost being forced into marriage with a horrid reprobate.

Fresh humiliation stabbed Jessica, and she swallowed. Or tried to. Her throat truly was dry.

She'd make sure to drink a glass of lemonade before her waltz with the duke, else she'd not be able to converse without croaking worse than the amorous amphibian in the garden.

"There you are."

2

Jessica glanced toward the speaker. A pretty, dark-haired, plump young woman approached, carrying two glasses in her fine-boned hands. Lemonade or ratafia?

Searching behind her for a chaperone and finding none, Jessica offered a genial smile. It seemed she wasn't the only one to brave a bit of censure by venturing outdoors alone. "I'm sorry, but I don't believe we've been introduced."

The girl—for she couldn't be much more than seventeen or eighteen—shook her head, causing her pearl-and-emerald earrings to bob. A mischievous glint in her eyes—were they brown?—she made an exaggerated pretense of inspecting the area. "We haven't. But I shan't tell if you don't."

Jessica liked her instantly. "I'm Jessica Brentwood."

Blast. Another faux pas. Introducing oneself wasn't *de rigueur*. She was supposed to find someone who knew the other woman and ask them to do the honors—a silly waste of time.

"I'm Lilith Brighton," the girl said, offering one of the glasses.

Jessica wasn't familiar with the name, but that wasn't a surprise. As this was her first week in London, she knew few people. A quick inspection of the cloudy liquid, and she dubbed it lemonade.

"I saw you earlier," Miss Brighton said. Then her forehead puckered, and she turned her mouth down. "And, I fear, I couldn't help but overhear what those malicious twits said about your father. I suspected you'd intended to relieve your thirst, so after I gave them a piece of my mind, I set out in search of you. Please believe me when I tell you not everyone is as shallow or judgmental as they are."

Gratitude suffused Jessica that this stranger would champion her and had even realized she'd been thirsty and come looking for her with lemonade, too.

She racked her memory.

Had Miss Brighton been nearby when she'd gone in search of a beverage? Mayhap. After hearing the unkind conversation, Jessica had been quite upset. Miss Brighton might've been standing within an arm's reach, dressed as an Amazonian warrior, and Jessica wouldn't have noticed.

Her only thought had been to put as much distance as possible between herself and the vile gossipmongers before she said or did something that would add more fodder to the inferno that was her family's reputation.

Despite her determination, otherwise, Jessica had a bit of a quick temper when provoked. But only when provoked. Tonight, she most assuredly had been.

"Have you seen the darling puppies yet?" Miss Brighton cheerily asked, trailing her attention around the terrace and gardens before bringing that inquisitive gaze back to her.

Jessica adored animals, as anyone who knew her

at all could attest. Particularly baby animals. "Puppies?"

She took a long, grateful sip of the lemonade. Gracious, it was tart, but also very welcome to her dry mouth and throat. Not everyone liked the citrusy drink as sweet as she preferred. In fact, Mama had claimed plain lemon water a curative, though they seldom had the funds to spend on the fruit.

Grinning, Miss Brighton nodded eagerly, her attention once more sweeping the area.

Was she afraid of being caught outdoors?

Perhaps she wasn't as bold as Jessica had first thought, which made her efforts to find her all that much more generous. However, as they were in each other's company now, no one could proclaim them improper.

"Oh, yes. The Duke of Westfall's grandmother's Pomeranian had three precious puppies a fortnight ago. They're absolutely *adorable*." She scrunched her nose and drew out the word. "She so dotes on the dog. Treats her like a pampered child. My parents have said that I might have one if—"

A shadow passed over her round face but quickly disappeared, replaced by her bubbly countenance once more.

Two gentlemen tripped down the steps to the garden below, and a moment later, one lit a cheroot. He angled in the terrace's direction briefly before they wandered away along one of the serpentine pathways, their footsteps crunching on the gravel. At the far end of the porch, three couples made a slow turn, the ladies briskly waving their fans before their faces to create a breeze.

The ballroom must've become more unbearably warm, for more attendees had braved the less-than-hospitable outdoors. Their numbers would likely increase as the evening wore on.

However, it had grown impossibly cooler in the past five minutes, and Jessica had become quite chilled. She should probably go back inside before she was missed and before she became any colder.

After draining her glass, she set the etched crystal on the balustrade, her thirst not quite quenched. A drink of water wouldn't go amiss, but she'd yet to sample water in London as fresh as that in Colechester.

Miss Brighton placed her half-full cup beside Jessica's.

"Come, I'll show you. They're in the conservatory." She sliced Jessica another friendly grin. "Well, it's too small to be a real conservatory. But there are several lush plants, a fountain in the center, and a pair of settees and few chairs scattered about. It's quite charming."

Jessica hesitated. She'd been absent for several minutes already.

She spared a glance toward the house. Through the windows and open doors, she made out the shapes of a few dancers and the black-clad shoulder of one violinist. She'd be wise to seek the retiring room, too, to make sure the slight breeze hadn't loosened any of her hair from its pins.

Ruffled hair might give the wrong impression.

Ophelia and Theadosia might very well be looking for her by now. Jessica had been outside for several minutes already.

But she adored animals, and a chance to see

puppies greatly tempted. She missed her chickens—the *girls,* as she called them. Silly to have pet chickens, but she'd had chickens since she was eight years old.

The Season would be over soon enough, and then she could return to Colechester and her pets. Well, to Ridgefield Court. That's where she lived now, in a house grander than this one.

Though not yet eleven of the clock, she smothered a yawn. Theadosia said the ball might very well last until early morning. Accustomed to country hours, Jessica already felt the initial hindrance of fatigue. In truth, she preferred staying up late at night and sleeping in to mid-morning, but that lifestyle didn't suit in the country.

"How long will it take? Jessica asked. "My next dance is promised."

"Not more than five or ten minutes, I shouldn't think." Miss Brighton pointed to the building beyond the gardens. "It's just there. I'd love for you to help me pick which puppy I ought to choose. They are all so sweet. It's impossible to decide."

How could she refuse? "All right," Jessica

conceded, with another swift glance to the humming ballroom. “I can spare five minutes, I suppose.”

Miss Brighton’s effervescent demeanor was a welcome change, and Jessica could use another friend. Especially one who wasn’t afraid to take on vipers in her defense. “I wonder if I might convince my brother-in-law to permit me a puppy, as well?”

She’d adore a dog of her own. Her hens were sweet, but one couldn’t very well cuddle a chicken in bed, nor have it sleep on her lap. And, *dear heavens*, she couldn’t imagine trying to housetrain the girls.

“Oh, wouldn’t that be splendid? We could walk them in Hyde Park or Green Park together.” Miss Brighton fairly simmered with enthusiasm.

Her enthusiasm seemed a trifle overdone, but perhaps that was her nature. Jessica and Theadosia had never been what one would call high-spirited, and Miss Brighton was the epitome of exuberance and impetuousness.

It only took a couple of minutes to reach the hothouse. After a bit of fumbling with and grumbling at the uncooperative latch, Miss Brighton managed to open the door. She and Jessica slipped inside the considerably warmer building. Only a faint coolness tainted the air.

A single glowing lamp reposed upon a table between two mint-green divans situated in an L-shape. Arranged in clusters on the far side sat several healthy potted trees and plants. Between them, a trio of beautifully painted screens depicting exotic landscapes added vibrant color.

"I didn't think the latch was going to give, and I feared we wouldn't be able to see the little darlings," Miss Brighton said with a short, tense laugh. She pointed to a shadowy corner behind one screen. "They're over there."

The mother hadn't even barked upon their entrance. Either she was calm-natured, or she was asleep. "I'm surprised they aren't kept in the house, given, as you say, the dowager duchess is so fond of her pet."

Miss Brighton's sunny smile faltered, and she shifted her gaze to the side before lifting a shoulder. She plucked at the dance card dangling from her wrist.

"Ah, well…ah, they usually are. But I suppose…ah, with the commotion of the ball…"

Jessica would've removed them to a quiet bedchamber rather than the conservatory. The puppies might become chilled out here. Then again, there was no accounting for the eccentricities of the nobility.

She stepped forward then stumbled as severe dizziness overcame her.

Good Lord. I feel so peculiar. She held perfectly still, willing the unsteadiness to leave.

Pressing a palm to her forehead, she closed her eyes, trying to regain her equilibrium. The tilting increased to a frenzy, and her thoughts became muddled.

Why was she here again?

Oh, yes. To see puppies.

Why had it become so difficult to concentrate? She blinked several times, attempting to clear her vision and focus her thoughts.

"Miss Brentwood?" Miss Brighton's voice, hollow and distant, permeated the dense fog enshrouding her mind. "Are you quite well? You look about to swoon."

"No, I don't believe I am. I feel most irregular." Jessica swayed. "So dizzy." Her head felt thick and wooly. Her limbs weighty and cumbersome. Her thoughts sluggish and incoherent. "I…cannot…think…"

Speaking was becoming difficult, her words hard to form and thick upon her swollen tongue.

Was this the vapors?

But she'd never swooned in her life.

What had triggered an episode now?

"Permit me to assist you to the divan." All solicitousness and concern, Miss Brighton snaked an arm about Jessica's waist. "It's just here. A few more steps. Be careful."

Jessica forced her leaden legs to shuffle forward as Miss Brighton unerringly guided her to the seat.

"Here we are. You may sit now. Slowly." She gently urged Jessica down, her voice seemingly reaching through a long tunnel. "Sit back. There you are."

Releasing a grateful sigh, Jessica sank onto the welcoming cushions and promptly shut her eyes. The mad swirling didn't stop. In fact, the frenzy spiraling increased. Spinning and whirling, a muddled tornado of confusion and light-headedness.

"Shall I go for help?" The divan dipped as Miss Brighton sat beside her and took her hand. "Miss Brentwood? Can you hear me?"

It was simply too much effort to answer. Too dashed difficult to open her eyes. Her head spun round and round and round. Sounds and sensations faded and receded. Diminished, waning farther and farther away. She floated, spiraling into vast darkness.

What is happening?

That was her last coherent thought before blackness claimed her.

3

Crispin tossed back his last swallow of champagne and returned the nod Mathias, Duke of Westfall, sent him from farther along this side of the ballroom. Earlier, they'd discussed horseflesh—a stud Westfall wanted, to be precise. Depositing the empty flute on the tray a passing black-and-crimson-liveried footman carried, he casually surveyed the milling crowd, seeking Jessica Brentwood.

He'd dared to claim a waltz with her, although his common sense rebuffed him for the foolish impulse. Sutcliffe had asked him to dance with his sister-in-law, and Crispin was only too willing to honor his friend's request. Never mind that notion had been at the forefront of his mind since he'd ascended the steps to the house.

Laughing, Nicolette Twistleton and Ophelia Breckensole, along with Rayne Wellbrook and Justina Farthington, hurried from the ballroom. Ladies never seemed to be able to seek the retiring room unless they did so *en masse*.

It made him grateful to have been born a male.

Across the way, near an elaborate column, the Dukes of Pennington, Kincade, and Asherford engaged in earnest conversation. Victor, the Duke of Sutcliffe, danced with his duchess, as did the Dukes of Dandridge and Sheffield. Each was nauseatingly content in their wedded state, and he couldn't help but envy them.

If compelled down the marital path forced upon him at present, Crispin would leave his duchess at his remotest estate while taking himself off to India. Or China. Or the Americas, regularly. He and Lilith Brighton were as compatible as oil and water, and he'd be damned if he'd impose his presence on her or hers upon him.

Even his closest friends didn't know of his less-than-gallant intentions. He rather suspected they'd point out how unbecoming cowardice was, as well as abandoning one's spouse. Except, he wouldn't precisely be abandoning Lilith. She'd want for nothing, and he would have to return to England annually, at the minimum, to inspect his properties.

Chagrin chafed him, and he glared at the chalked floor. It wasn't her fault that he felt nothing for her and never would. His heart was too full of another.

Earlier in the day, he'd learned the Sutcliffe household was to attend the Westfalls' ball this evening, and he'd immediately altered his plans so he might see Jessica. It wasn't the first time he'd done so, which made him a complete assling. But as long as no one else suspected his *tendre*, he'd continue to do so.

Miss Jessica Brentwood was an enchantress and had consumed his musings for months. He'd secretly admired her from afar for as long. Nonetheless, he'd been diligent not to make overtures or give anyone cause for gossip or speculation.

After all, he was betrothed.

Not, *by God*, of his own free will.

And that frustration chafed raw and sharp. Gnawed at his peace and kept his mind in a constant turmoil. He did not desire the union with Lilith Brighton. Never had. Never would. How was he to escape the cursed match?

No, the real difficulty was dissolving the contract without ruining lives.

What about my life?

Somehow, he must make it so. He'd oppose the forced marriage until he'd exhausted every avenue.

The settlement had been drawn up when he was but a lad of twelve. At the time, he'd had no idea what his father had rushed him into signing. He'd wanted the deed done so he might return to the stables and to his best friend—a sweet-natured gelding named Ross.

His father had ordered him to put his name to the official-looking document, and so he had. One did not argue with the intimidating, formidable previous Duke of Bainbridge. Most especially not skinny, pimply-faced heirs whose fathers only deigned to criticize and find fault with everything they did.

Since coming into his title seven years ago, at the age of twenty, Crispin had consulted his solicitor in multiple instances regarding the intricacies of flouting the agreement. Unfortunately, the consequences would be most unpleasant, particularly if both parties were not amenable to the dissolution. The drafters of the contract had been cunning and wily. *Damn their eyes.*

It wasn't their lives being manipulated.

Personally, he didn't mind scandals too terribly much—if a scandal meant avoiding a union he deplored. Decades with a woman not of his choosing was, in essence, a lifetime prison sentence for a crime he hadn't committed.

Crispin glanced around the milling crowd, wishing he dared take a hefty swallow from the flask in his pocket. Ruminations of his impending marriage always made him want to get foxed.

Several years ago, his mother had married a widower with two grown sons and after the death of her husband, lived contentedly as the Dowager Baroness Waverly. Nevertheless, destroying Albertina's and Lettice's prospects wouldn't make him a hero in her—or his cossetted and indulged sisters'—eyes.

Right now, he didn't much care what they thought of him, truth be told.

While their dowries were sufficient to attract numerous suitors, they had, regrettably, taken after Waverly in form, intelligence, and disposition. Though he loved his sisters and wished them the best, given they were turnip-shaped, scatter-brained, and given to fits of temper and histrionics, neither would readily find herself a husband.

Perhaps they'd mature, adopt more biddable temperaments, before their Come Outs. At fourteen and fifteen, that wasn't entirely impossible. And neither was Prinny losing two stone and putting aside his mistresses. Just improbable as hell.

An eruption of high-pitched giggles behind him dragged him back to the present.

Crispin scrutinized the guests again before returning to the matter plaguing him. The ever-present burr in his bum, which permitted him no relaxation.

When the betrothal contract had been drafted

fifteen years ago, the duchy was nearly destitute. Since he'd come into the title, he'd made several lucrative investments, and now the dukedom sailed along quite smoothly. He couldn't afford to be unwise, but if he stayed the course, his heir wouldn't bear the same financial trials that had burdened him upon inheriting the dukedom.

Money wasn't the only issue, however. Years before, Crispin had repaid the funds advanced to the duchy. Well, he'd had his solicitor deposit the funds in Hammon Brighton's account.

What was trickier to negotiate was the property Father had acquired in the agreement. Property upon which sat the house he had commissioned and which Mother and his sisters now resided.

Not only was it forfeit if Crispin broke the agreement, but Brighton was also guaranteed two other unentailed estates, including Pickford Hill Park, where Crispin conducted his horse-breeding ventures. The reverse was true if Lilith Brighton, his intended, refused the match. All the properties remained Crispin's holdings.

By damn, Brighton would *not* put his grubby paws on Pickford Hill Park.

However, Crispin still hadn't contrived a suitable solution to the betrothal.

Lilith had recently celebrated her eighteenth birthday. The agreed-upon age when he and she would exchange vows. Since that auspicious day had come and gone, his mother and Lilith's father nagged worse than fishwives for Crispin to set a wedding date. Soon. Before Season's end, by God. He could feel the noose tightening more and more with each passing day.

"Ballocks," he swore beneath his breath.

He didn't fool himself that his mother's concern was for him. She'd never been an affectionate woman. Her union with Father had been arranged, and there'd been no love between them. She fretted that his pampered sisters would have to leave their preferred home. And Albertina and Lettice *always* demanded and usually had their way.

Which, until now, had suited him fine. As long as they didn't take up residence at Pickford Hill Park, he didn't give a dozen damns where they lived. Pray God, he wouldn't be required to assist with their Come Outs.

A shudder rippled across his shoulders at the horrifying notion. God save him from such cruel punishment.

Bored, Crispin took in the revelers again.

Where the blazes was Miss Brentwood?

His affianced was also in attendance tonight. Strangely, the moment she'd spied him, she'd flown from the ballroom, apparently no more thrilled to see him than he'd been to see her. He felt neither offended nor pleased at the knowledge. In truth, Lilith Brighton stirred no emotion, or anything else, in him. His intended was little more than a cossetted child.

Crispin hadn't bothered to determine if she'd returned to the ballroom yet.

He had no intention of asking her to dance. He didn't want to encourage Lilith. Young women too easily fell in and out of infatuation. Far better for all if she remained leery of him as he pondered a means of dissolving their marriage contract.

Sighing, he scrubbed a hand over his chin. Physical fatigue didn't cause his weariness, but rather mental exhaustion. If only there were an honorable way to put an end to their betrothment. Mayhap he could persuade Lilith to terminate it or, together, come to an amicable settlement for dissolution.

Not bloody likely.

Weren't all marriage-minded misses eager to become a duchess? Shallow ones such as Lilith most assuredly were. Except her behavior tonight said otherwise.

It mattered naught. Her social-climbing father, Hammon Brighton, would never consent. He'd purchased their daughter a title, and now Crispin and Miss Lilith Brighton must somehow forge a future together that neither had chosen.

He'd spoken to her father, and the blackguard had made it most clear; his daughter *would* become a duchess. More specifically, the Duchess of Bainbridge. Or there would be hell to pay.

Nevertheless, Crispin wasn't leg-shackled yet, and he'd damn well enjoy his dance with Jessica Brentwood.

"Bainbridge?" Ronald, Viscount Brookmoore,

approached, yanking him once more from his unpleasant musings. His aristocratic features tense, Brookmoore glanced around before lowering his voice. “Might I impose upon you to assist me with my brother? Inconspicuously?”

A sot and a rakehell of the worst order, Randolph Radcliff was notorious for becoming embroiled in one disgraceful conundrum after another.

Crispin cocked an eyebrow. “What’s he up to now?”

“He’s foxed to his gills.” Brookmoore made a sound of disgust. “Drank nearly a half bottle of Scotch before we left home, and God only knows how much he’s consumed since.”

And Brookmoore asked *him* to help? Why not one of his usual cronies?

The viscount must’ve anticipated the question. “I require a man of some…ah…discretion to assist in bundling my brother into our carriage. It’s parked outside the alley, by the garden. For my family’s sake, I’d rather not ask the footmen to help. You know how servants gossip.” He gave a rueful twist of his lips and shook his head. "Mother hasn't recovered entirely from the last debacle."

Was that the one where Radcliffe had been caught with the maid in the linen closet, her skirts over her head? Or the episode with the new-to-London widow whose very-much-alive husband had returned home at the most inopportune moment? *Egads.* Radcliffe made him grateful he only had stout sisters with difficult temperaments to deal with.

"I'd be most appreciative," Brookmoore murmured, brushing a hand over his weak chin while surreptitiously examining the company. "You don't gossip as many do, and I know I can rely upon your circumspection."

With a sharp nod, Crispin angled toward the doors leading onto the terrace. As the Duke of Westfall was a good friend, he was well-acquainted with the grounds. A gate exited directly to the mew's alley from the garden. Quite convenient for furtively removing foxed dandies from the premises.

Aiding Brookmoore also provided him an opportunity to take a nip from the flask in his pocket.

He required something stiffer than lukewarm champagne or weak punch suitable for tipsy tabbies. His discussion earlier in the evening with the blissfully happy, newlywed Pennington hadn't improved his sour mood either.

Four of his closest friends—Dandridge, Sutcliffe, Sheffield, and now Pennington—had managed to marry for love. They'd found women that complimented them and made them into better men. No wonder he felt disgruntled at the woman foisted upon him.

Miss Brighton was attractive enough, he supposed. Quite pretty actually, if a man preferred empty-headed, dark-haired, brown-eyed fashionable dolls. However, the few occasions they'd spoken—when he'd been trapped with no ready escape—she'd babbled inanely about lace and buttons and rose water. Kittens. Tea. Oh, and Lady Wimpleton's *divine* tea cakes.

There'd also been envious tripe about somebody's betrothal. Even a gloating whisper regarding the scandalous crimson gown somebody-or-other had worn to…*something*.

A ball? Rout? Theater? *Funeral?*

By that time, Crispin had so detached himself from the conversation, preferring to have his eyes gouged out with a salt spoon rather than attend to her nattering, he wouldn't have recalled if she'd declared Almack's patronesses had paraded through Hyde Park, wearing nothing but peacock feathers in their hair and bells on their toes.

"I'm afraid my brother has become the bane of our dear mother's existence," Brookmoore was mumbling when Crispin stopped his ruminations and, once more, focused on the viscount.

"You really ought to do something about his drinking, Brookmoore. Cut off his allowance, if you must. Have him banned from his clubs." Disgust riddled him. When deep in his cups, Radcliff became boisterous and obnoxious. No woman was safe from his groping hands. "If he keeps on this dubious track, he'll have a pickled liver by the time he's thirty."

A hand on his pocket, prepared to withdraw his flask, Crispin paused. He'd be obligated to offer Brookmoore a swig. Best wait until he'd seen the viscount and his errant brother on their way.

Heaving a gusty sigh, Brookmoore fell into step beside him. “You’re right, of course. I’m considering sending him to the Continent. At least, there, his antics wouldn’t constantly embarrass the family.”

Crispin gave a noncommittal grunt. That might be worse. Brookmoore would have no control over his brother, and God only knew what the pup would embroil himself in. Besides, Brookmoore’s behavior wasn’t exactly above reproach.

In truth, Crispin had only agreed to aid him to prevent anything untoward happening at Westfalls’ ball.

A minute later, they trotted down the terrace steps, their heels softly clacking on the stones. Sure enough, the polished ebony top of a coach glinted above the garden wall directly beside the gate.

Several other guests’ equipages also lined the alley.

Raising his face to inhale the reviving air, he eyed the cloud-scattered, inky sky. Moonbeams sliced through branches laden with plump buds. Spring hovered, ready to burst forth in a week or two. "Let's be about it, then. I have a waltz I don't wish to miss."

Slicing him a wolfish glance, Brookmoore scratched his temple. "A little dallying before committing yourself to the parson's mousetrap, eh? I take it you don't intend to keep yourself only to your Miss Brighton, despite her sizable dowry? A veritable fortune, I hear. If I were you, I'd not want to anger her dear papa. He might tighten the purse strings."

Was that a note of criticism in his voice? *Him?* A known rakehell? Talk about the proverbial pot calling the kettle black.

Brookmoore made Prinny look like a monk. How many mistresses had he gone through this past year alone? *Seven? Eight?* The poor woman who found herself Viscountess Brookmoore had better have a physician examine her for the clap. Monthly.

Brookmoore wasn't at all particular in the feminine company he kept.

Tightening his jaw to quash his instinctive terse retort, Crispin glanced overhead again. "I'm sure you're aware the match was arranged when I was a mere lad." He needn't explain his personal business, though the underlying details weren't a secret. "I'm unconvinced it's the best course for me to continue to pursue."

A guarded expression descended onto Brookmoore's features, appearing almost sinister in the half-light, with the tree branches casting weird shadows over them. "But how do you intend to avoid…?"

Fishing, was he?

"That, I don't know, as of yet." A sardonic chuckle escaped Crispin. "I'd rather there wasn't a scandal. It would be much better for all, including Miss Brighton. I wish no disgrace or discomfort upon her. She's a pawn as much as I."

Hands linked behind his back, Brookmoore merely grunted.

They'd reached the conservatory, and he opened the door, permitting Crispin to enter first.

He stopped short.

Pale and nervously wringing her hands and biting her lower lip, Miss Brighton stood beside the fountain.

Something akin to relief flitted over her face upon spying them.

Why, in blazes, was she here?

He fired an accusing glare toward Brookmoore.

"What's this? Miss Brighton, why—?" He started forward, but a woman lying prostrate on a divan snared his attention. He blinked once, not believing his eyes. "*Miss Brentwood*?"

His brows lashed together in alarm. *What the devil?* His nape hair stood straight up as alarm bells pealed loudly in his head. Why was Jessica here, incapacitated, and Radcliffe—the bounder—obviously was not?

Brookmoore had lied. Fabricated the whole bloody story.

But, *God's teeth*, why?

Something was too deuced smoky by far.

"Where's your brother, Brookmoore?" Crispin snapped, shooting the disconcertingly silent man a half accusing, half questioning glance as he strode to Jessica.

What drivel would he concoct?

He knelt beside the divan. "Miss Brentwood?" He gave her shoulder a gentle shake, but she didn't stir. Didn't so much as twitch. What the hell went on?

How long had she been in the hothouse? If she didn't return to the ball soon, she faced inevitable ruination. He raked an accusatory gaze over Miss Brighton, who'd skirted the divan to stand before the door. No, to stand beside Brookmoore.

She was Crispin's affianced, yet he felt more concern and regard for the insensate woman on the divan than he did for her. "What's wrong with her?" he demanded, stonily. His taut gut told him Miss Brighten knew full well what ailed Jessica.

When she didn't answer but flicked her anxious gaze to Brookmoore, Crispin firmed his lips together. Did affection soften the worried lines about her mouth?

Ah, so that was which way the wind blew. Ire replaced his satisfaction with the discovery. Those two fiends were behind this…whatever the bloody nuisance this was.

By God, he'd get to the bottom, but first, he must

ascertain what was wrong with Jessica. His betrothed and Brookmoore had a great deal of explaining to do.

He touched Jessica's forehead with the back of his hand, relieved when he detected no fever. Her chest rose and fell, her breathing even and unlabored. She appeared peaceful and deeply asleep. She hadn't responded to their talk nor when he touched her.

Drugged. Jessica acted drugged.

Hell's bells! He jerked his head up, prepared to give Brookmoore and Miss Brighton a tongue lashing requiring a fortnight's recovery. "Precisely what—"

Excruciating pain lanced the base of Crispin's skull. He toppled forward, collapsing atop Jessica's bountiful chest.

A woman gasped, the sound muffled and appalled. "Ronny! You might've killed him."

His vision grew narrower and narrower until the last vestige of light disappeared.

4

Crispin groaned, his skull threatening to crack with the harsh, guttural sound. He touched his fingertips to the bridge of his nose, applying pressure to ease the hammering in his head.

What the hell had happened?

He'd recalled bending over Jessica, and then—

Goddammit. Brookmoore had walloped the back of his head.

The whole thing had been a calculated ploy. But why?

Was Jessica part of the scheme, or was she a victim, too?

He dropped his hand to his naked chest. *Naked?*

Why was he naked?

Fingers splayed, he waited for his mind to catch up to the undeniable evidence beneath his palm. It took another second for him to comprehend he was completely unclothed. Nude as the day he'd been born.

Shit. Shit. Shit.

And what was more—*God dammit!*—he wasn't alone on the divan. His breath hissed out from between his teeth, and every muscle in his torso tensed.

Could things possibly become any worse?

A lush feminine body curled into his, a slim thigh thrown across his legs and a slender arm across his bare chest. The tantalizing scents of cloves and vanilla surrounded him as he slowly turned his head, dreading yet knowing, he'd find Jessica Brentwood in his arms. Also deliciously naked as a robin, her honey-blonde hair splayed over her shoulders and back.

He might've been knocked senseless and still struggled to cobble a coherent thought together, but he was aware enough to appreciate the exquisiteness of the form tucked so intimately next to his. Like a contented kitten.

She made a soft noise and shivered, burrowing deeper into his side, and despite his head threatening to split at the slightest movement, desire sluiced through him. She was even more incredibly beautiful than he'd imagined. And he *had* imagined her naked—many, *many* times.

He supposed that made him a bounder and a reprobate. *God rot me.* But, despite what others believed, it wasn't something he did with all women. Just this special, unique creature.

Jessica's unbound golden hair fell over her creamy shoulders, and her bountiful breasts pressed enticingly against his chest, her delectably plump buttocks sloping downward to long, lithe legs.

To anyone coming upon them, it would appear they recovered from a rousing round of satiating love play. Damn his eyes. He would kill Brookmoore—*slowly*—for looking upon Jessica and touching her.

He squinted through half-closed lids, the pounding in his head preventing him from opening his eyes wide. When he'd entered the hothouse, a single lamp had burned on the table. Now, however, three more glowed brightly. Someone had gone to a great deal of trouble to make it appear as if he and Jessica had just coupled. To compromise and entrap them.

Lilith.

The devious, little bitch.

Rage such as he'd never known pummeled behind his ribs and boiled his blood. If it weren't for his cracking headache and the woman nestled beside him, he'd have been up, dressed, and in furious pursuit. No doubt, Lilith and Brookmoore had counted on his being incapacitated for some time. They'd ensured it by bashing him on the head.

That bastard Brookmoore and his witch of a betrothed would feel the full effect of his wrath. He was typically much better at reading people and cursed himself for being ten times a fool for being so damn gullible.

Concern for Jessica had dulled his instincts.

His question as to whether she was as bitterly opposed to the match between them as Crispin, had been answered. Once she'd turned eighteen and knew a wedding date was forthcoming, Lilith had determined to take matters into her own hands.

Why hadn't she approached her father? Mayhap she had.

Brighton wouldn't have given ten tinkers' damns about her feelings. He'd already proved that. So, Lilith had used other nefarious means to achieve her end. It seems his betrothed—*former* betrothed, after this unforgivable stunt—was a cunning, plotting witch.

As awful as the situation was at present, at least he'd learned the truth about her.

But why in the hell had Brookmoore schemed to help her? Unless…

Ah. Of course.

He wanted Lilith for himself. Wanted her fortune-of-a-marriage-settlement.

Did they think Crispin wouldn't bring charges against them? If Brookmoore had gambled he wouldn't drag him before the House of Lords, he'd gambled wrong. Or had Brookmoore and Lilith truly intended to kill him? Crispin intended to find out, by God.

He would obliterate him for disrobing Jessica, looking upon her naked form, and touching her. Fury throttled up his throat, and he gritted his teeth. He damn well might challenge Brookmoore to an affair of honor.

However, despite Jessica being a victim too, she was thoroughly and undeniably compromised. Even if whatever had caused her insensate condition was proven, the facts were the facts.

They were naked. Together.

It didn't matter that nothing had occurred between them. That he was injured, and she was unconscious. Or that he wasn't in any condition to rouse her, let alone see them both into their clothing.

Shutting his eyes, he battled the waves of nausea assailing him. He swallowed, willing the contents of his stomach to stay where they were. Vomiting on Jessica wouldn't endear him to her.

Brookmoore may very well have concussed him. Gingerly, Crispin touched the back of his head, unsurprised when his fingertips came away sticky with blood. The blow that damned wretch dealt him had left a gash in his skull.

He wiped his fingers on the back of the divan then

grimaced at the bloody smears. Westfall's mother would not be pleased.

Had Lilith and Brookmoore contrived this debacle to place the blame on Crispin by causing the scandal of the year? He'd wager on it. Had Brookmoore already bedded Lilith?

Probably.

Which meant, if Crispin's hunch proved right—and by God and all of the saints, he was positive it would—someone would burst through the door any moment. And most conveniently find him and Jessica *dishabille*.

Perhaps he should feign unconsciousness again to lend credence to the truth that they'd been set up. He skimmed his gaze over her creamy skin, and his instinct to protect her won over. No others would have an opportunity to leer at her when she was defenseless. She'd be utterly humiliated.

She would be, in any event. There was no help for it.

"Jessica. Jessica." Gently but firmly shaking her shoulders, he whispered in her ear, "You must wake up, sweetheart."

God help them. She didn't revive except to sigh and press her lush curves closer, reinforcing his suspicion she'd been drugged.

How much time had passed? *Minutes? Hours?*

God damn Lilith and Brookmoore to the lowest layer of hell. May they burn for eternity.

How could they involve Jessica? An innocent. She'd done nothing to either of them to warrant this type of hostile treatment.

She'd be utterly compromised. Destroyed. Shunned through no fault of her own.

Brookmoore or Lilith had probably heard the ugly tattle about Jessica's father and decided she was expendable. A woman with a slightly-tainted reputation by association. They'd targeted the weak, and that only made Crispin all the more determined to seek revenge on Jessica's behalf.

Murderous fury burgeoned within him, wave after wave of ire so blistering that if Brookmoore had been present, he'd have run him through on the spot.

Through slitted eyelids, Crispin located their

clothing, scattered haphazardly beside the settee. Lilith and Brookmoore had been in an all-fired hurry to disrobe them, the fiends. The garments were tossed about as if he and Jessica had been frantic to couple.

Her gown was within reach, and stretching out an arm, he managed to seize the fine silk as voices rang outside. With a jerk that threatened to separate his head from his shoulders, he yanked the gown over them, concealing their nudity a fraction before the door flung open and several laughing guests paraded in.

A chorus of stunned gasps and exclamations echoed throughout the hothouse as they came up short, bumping into one another.

"I say," Radcliffe boomed with mock astonishment. "It's Bainbridge and the Brentwood chit."

"Good Lord," his female companion tittered. "And they're *naked*."

5

Jessica groaned and rolled over, pressing a hand to her throbbing head. The last thing she remembered was feeling wretched in the Westfalls' hothouse. She swallowed, her mouth dry as ash and tasting of soiled linen. And mayhap feathers. No, a dirty feather duster.

Why had she been in the conservatory, again?

The details flitted around the periphery of her memory, almost within her grasp then darting away each time she nearly had them in her grip.

Puppies.

Yes, she'd gone to see puppies with Lilith Brighton. But she'd become dizzy and fainted. For the first time in her life, and for no apparent reason, she'd swooned. It was all so peculiar.

Opening her eyes, she peered at the familiar emerald canopy above her.

Puzzling her brow and crimping her mouth, she rifled through her inadequate recollections of last night. How in heaven's name had she come to be in her bed and not recall the journey home from the Westfalls'?

Turning onto her side, her mind still in a thick-as-cold-porridge muddle, she examined the draperies. Bright, golden light filtered between the small crack. Morning, then. She'd been unconscious all night.

Suspicion niggled. A simple bout of the vapors didn't cause one to remain incapacitated for hours. Jessica became more confused with each passing moment. *What*, precisely, had happened last night?

Struggling to a sitting position, she groaned again at the fierce ache encompassing her skull like an unyielding vise. Once propped against her pillows, she cradled her head in her hands. This aftermath was most definitely something more than a simple swoon.

Tap. Tap. Tap.

Faint, almost tentative knocking preceded Theadosia gliding into the bedchamber, followed by a maid with a breakfast tray.

"You're awake, at last. I'm so very relieved." At once, Theadosia sat beside her on the mattress and took Jessica's hands in hers. "Even though the doctor assured me you—"

"Doctor?" Jessica cut a bewildered glance at Sally, in the process of setting out breakfast and pouring a cup of tea. The servant's ears practically flapped as she listened, though her bland expression never changed.

"That will be all, Sally." Theadosia rose, and head tilted regally, waited expectantly for the maid to depart.

Ah, so Theadosia wanted privacy before she filled Jessica in on what had happened last evening. A bit curious, but not alarming.

Sally bobbed a shallow curtsy. "Yes, Your Grace." She left the chamber, closing the door with a soft *thud* behind her, but not before cutting Jessica another curiosity-filled glance.

Theadosia took her place at the table, fiddling with

the tea service. She added milk and a lump of sugar to Jessica's cup and, after stirring the tea, brought her the fragrant brew.

India tea was her favorite, and this morning more than usual, she welcomed the soothing beverage. She took a sip, relishing the sweet warmth trickling down her throat. A fortifying cup of tea did much to set the world to rights.

If Theadosia didn't look like she was about to cast up her accounts, Jessica wouldn't be troubled. Her sister was with child, after all, so perhaps her wan expression was due to morning sickness.

"Are you feeling unwell? I thought your morning malaise had passed."

"What?" Her sister stared at her in bafflement before her expression cleared. "Oh, no. Not at all. I feel perfectly well," she assured her. "That is, I'm not ill in the stomach."

"Then why the Friday-face?" Jessica took another sip. She felt much improved already. "And what's this about a doctor? I but fainted." That might not be entirely true. Mayhap she had a debilitating ailment, and that's why Theadosia acted so oddly. "Did Miss Brighton send for help? Well, naturally, she must've, else I'd still be in the conservatory."

When her sister didn't respond to her attempt at lightness, Jessica placed her cup upon her night table and canted her head.

Something *was* the matter.

Her chest expanded with a deep breath. Well, if there were something mortally wrong with her, she'd just as soon know. "What, precisely, did the doctor say, Theadosia?"

Cancer? Consumption? Some other nameless disease?

Apprehension sang through her veins, but she corralled her cavorting thoughts and presented a false mien of composure. Whatever Theadosia had to say that was so godawful, Jessica would face it courageously.

Her sister stood beside the bed, her upper teeth resting on her lower lip, her face pinched in consternation. "The doctor examined you last night, after the, ah, *incident*, and assured me once the sleeping draught wore off, you'd be fine."

Crumpling her brows in confusion, Jessica tried to make sense of her sister's words.

Sleeping draught? Incident? "I didn't take a sleeping draught." She shook her head and immediately regretted doing so when a pang speared her forehead. *Lord above.* "Why in the world would I need a sleeping draught at a ball? And what incident occurred?"

"My dear, you didn't knowingly drink the draught." Sighing deeply, Theadosia sank onto the mattress. "Did you accept a beverage from anyone?"

Miss Brighton's sunny countenance immediately sprang to mind, and she gave a cautious nod. "A glass of lemonade from—"

"Miss Brighton," her sister finished, staring past Jessica and gazing blankly out the window on the chamber's far side. Tension and, perhaps, regret radiated off her, and after a long, resigned sigh, she said, "Yes, I know. Or at least, I suspected that was the case."

Then, why had she asked? This conversation was

most peculiar.

"The Duke of Bainbridge suggested as much," Theadosia admitted, in a strangely distracted tone.

Now Jessica crinkled *her* nose. "The Duke of Bainbridge?"

How was he involved? What in the world had happened after she'd swooned? Had she hit her head? Was that why it ached as ferociously as if a hammer pounded an anvil inside her skull?

"Theadosia?" She touched her sister's cold hand. "You'll have to begin at the beginning, for I am hopelessly lost. What has Bainbridge to do with this? And what makes you think Miss Brighton would dose my lemonade? She was quite kind to me after…"

Jessica didn't finish. Theadosia needn't know about the viperish trio.

Come to think of it, though, the lemonade had been exceedingly tart. But her thirst had been such that she'd disregarded the flavor. A low gasp escaped past her parted lips. "The lemonade *did* taste rather peculiar."

The uncertainty gripping her rapidly transformed

into alarm at the devastation shining in Theadosia's eyes, at whatever unpleasantness her sister seemed unable to voice. It couldn't be all that dreadful. Could it?

Using two fingers, Jessica rubbed slow circles over her temples. Why would Miss Brighton drug her? It made no sense whatsoever.

"What…?" Dropping her hands to her lap, she swallowed past the lump of trepidation lodged in her throat. "What has happened?" She pressed her sister's fingers. "Tell me, Thea. I shall have to know eventually."

Her sister closed her eyes for a long blink, and when she opened them, moisture glimmered there. "Darling, you and the Duke of Bainbridge have been the unfortunate victims of an atrocious, simply malicious scheme."

"A scheme? Perpetuated by Miss Brighton?" Had she unknowingly offended the girl somehow? Unlikely, since Jessica was new to London and, until last night, had never laid eyes on the dark-haired vixen.

"Yes, and Lord Brookmoore. We believe they

eloped last night, for no one has seen them since they disappeared from the ball. It was some time before anyone noticed their absences. To throw the scent off their disgraceful intentions, the despicable rotters, they arranged for you and the duke to be found in a very indecent situation."

Jessica absently scratched her jaw, still uncertain why her sister was in such a dither. It wasn't like Theadosia in the least. "So…they created a scene to draw attention away from their clandestine disappearance?" Rather extreme and not just a little addled. "Why did they choose the duke and me?"

Pausing, Theadosia distractedly straightened her lace cuff. Instead of answering Jessica's question, she said, "You do know Miss Brighton and Bainbridge are—were—betrothed, don't you? Arrangements were made when they were children. She was an infant, I believe."

Atrocious practice, that. Marriages of convenience and arranged marriages between adults were awful enough.

"No, I wasn't aware." Something akin to envy

speared Jessica, but before she could examine the irregular emotion further, she forced herself to focus on the matter at hand. "But, be that as it may, the duke wasn't in the hothouse."

Had the whole lemonade episode been a farce, as well? Jessica suspected she already knew that ugly truth. Miss Brighton had probably been in cahoots with the other girls who'd been so unkind. She'd been play-acting. That was why her high-spirits had seemed somewhat affected.

"He *was* there. He arrived after you succumbed to the sleeping draught. We've puzzled the pieces together as best we can." Theadosia shifted, pulling one leg higher on the mattress, her lavender skirts rippling with the movement and thrusting her rounded belly forward. "After drugging you, Miss Brighton somehow lured you to the conservatory."

"She said there were puppies there, and she was to have one. I thought perhaps I might have one as well."

The devious, lying chit. Just wait until she had Miss Brighton alone. Her ears would ring for a month. Jessica might even slap her pretty face.

Hard.

"Ah." Understanding dawned in her sister's compassionate, brown-eyed gaze. "We did wonder since you have a level head on your shoulders, and we couldn't imagine you would rashly go off with her."

Why shouldn't she have trusted Miss Brighton? After all, she wasn't a thief or a woman of ill repute. Nothing of the sort. She'd been cheerful and friendly. A consummate actress.

"What happened after I lost consciousness?" It was worrisome that she had no recollection of anything between plopping onto the divan and waking up in her bed a few minutes ago.

Theadosia touched a finger to her chin, her eyes narrowed in concentration. "It's a bit garbled, but we've gleaned the duke was lured to the hothouse as well. Under the pretense of assisting Lord Brookmoore with his drunken brother. Radcliffe wasn't there, of course."

This entire scenario was as calamitous as a Drury Lane tragedy. Jessica would laugh if it weren't so disturbing. It didn't say much about her or Bainbridge that they were so gullible, either.

"His grace found you drugged on the divan and at once surmised foul play was afoot when he couldn't rouse you," Theadosia said, her manner hesitant and subdued. "Someone struck him in the back of the head with a brass candlestick, and when he awoke—"

6

"My God!" Jessica stiffened, anger rippling over her. "He might've been killed!"

Lips parted and rapidly blinking as if to stave off tears, Theadosia seemed unable to go on.

Jessica was afraid to ask how Crispin fared. What wasn't her sister telling her?

She scooted higher against the pillows, her stomach pitching worse than a skiff in a tropical hurricane. "Is Cris—that is, is the duke all right?"

Theadosia slowly nodded, though none of the tension left her face. "He will be. He required several stitches and suffered a concussion. The physician has ordered bed rest for a week. We've no doubt he speaks the truth about what he remembers."

Quite right. What man whacks himself on the back of the head so he can be found with a woman, even if he is a rake?

"I was drugged, and he was clobbered. Why? None of this makes any sense, and it certainly paints Miss Brighton and Lord Brookmoore as villains of the worst caliber." If Lilith were a man, she'd call her out, the wretch. How dare they conspire to ruin her and Crispin?

"They are, indeed." Theadosia nodded vehemently. "We're convinced—Victor, Bainbridge, and I—they acted so that Miss Brighton and Lord Brookmoore might elope. You and the duke were to be a distraction."

"There are easier ways to break a betrothal." Jessica released a contemptuous snort, her opinion of the bubbly Miss Brighton having descended to somewhere below a maggot in chicken manure. "I have decided I do not like Miss Brighton or Viscount Brookmoore in the least."

"Neither do I." The faintest smile curved

Theadosia's lips, though no humor lit her eyes. "They are utterly despicable, and their part in this debacle will not go unpunished. *However…*" Her tone changed, and she cinched her mouth tight.

Another wave of alarm engulfed Jessica, and she flashed cold. "What aren't you telling me?"

"Oh, darling." Droplets slipped from the corners of Theadosia's eyes. "Those monsters undressed you and Bainbridge and placed you in a *suggestive* position atop the divan. A half dozen guests found you together."

Undressed? Suggestive? Found by guests?

Oh God. Oh God, oh God!

Time stretched out, lengthening impossibly with disbelief and denial as Jessica sought to comprehend what her sister had said, the absolutely desolating consequences of what she'd disclosed.

Only the bedside clock's ticking punctuated the solemn silence.

"Thea, you're saying we were found *naked?* Together?" *Damn them.*

Humiliation blazed fiery heat up her cheeks.

Could a person perish from mortification?

No, but they could certainly want to.

Theadosia nodded, looking utterly miserable.

"And others *saw* us?" Jessica whispered, hands pressed to her flaming face.

No. No. No.

Her tummy toppled so violently that she feared she'd be sick all over her counterpane.

How could Lord Brookmoore and Miss Brighton have been so calculatingly malicious? Vile? Evil?

Scorching tears borne of chagrin, rage, and frustration sprang to her eyes. She'd do a great deal more than slap Lilith Brighton and the Lord Brookmoore when next she looked upon their despicable persons.

"Bainbridge managed to reach your gown and cover the essential parts of you both before the other guests barged in. Even injured and bleeding—barely conscious, the witnesses claim— he valiantly tried to protect you," her sister said, her voice tremulous with suppressed emotion.

Crispin had tried to preserve her modesty.

A little flicker of something undefinable fluttered behind Jessica's ribs. Perchance he wasn't the knave she'd believed him to be.

More likely, he didn't want a crowd viewing his man bits.

A flush swept her to think she'd been in his arms, naked, and assuredly, he'd seen her...*bits.* Felt her body, too. *God save me.* Jessica made a strangled sound, deep in her throat, which very much tried to become a moan. She'd never be able to look him in the face again. Never.

Theadosia withdrew a handkerchief from her bodice and patted her damp face. "Randolph Radcliffe was amongst the guests to discover you and the duke. We've no doubt he conspired with his dastardly brother. Though, as expected, he pleads absolute ignorance."

Devil take him. And the bubbly, black-hearted Miss Brighton, too.

Her sister's expression became steel-hard, and a flintiness entered her usually warm, chocolaty gaze. "Victor assures me he has the means to extract the truth from Radcliffe."

"God forgive me, but I sincerely hope it involves a degree of torture." Jessica emphasized her words with a vicious thwack to a pillow, which had the unfortunate fate of being nearby. "Tar and feathers or thumb screws, at the very least, the bloody bastard."

A raspy laugh escaped Theadosia, and she didn't even chide Jessica about her foul language. "No, nothing so medieval, more's the pity. Victor is buying all of his vowels and ensuring no one extends him credit. He'll be in no position to deny Victor anything."

Jessica fisted her hands in the sheets, her breath coming in shallow rasps. "What's to be done? I'm ruined," she whispered, bile's acrid burn stinging her throat.

Ruined? No, it was much worse than that. Despite her innocence, she'd be branded a whore. She'd have to leave London straightaway. Today, perhaps. And now, because of those selfish blighters, she'd probably never marry. What man would take a woman to wife who was found naked in public in another man's arms?

A scourge of stinging tears flooded her eyes again, and she shoved a fist to her mouth to stifle the cry of denial, throttling up her throat.

"The scandal will destroy you and Victor, too," she choked out.

"Victor and I are not concerned about any of that. We'll survive this storm, perhaps a little weather-beaten but not destroyed." Theadosia tenderly smoothed the hair away from Jessica's face, her closed-lip smile apologetic. "You and Bainbridge will wed. There's nothing else for it, my dear." Laced with sympathy and compassion, her sister's voice also held uncompromising authority.

Wed Crispin? A rake and a roué?

A man who could no more be faithful to one woman than fruit trees could retain their foliage in wintertime or snow could fall upward? *No.* There must be another solution. There *must* be. Marriage to him would guarantee a broken heart and a lifetime of unhappiness.

"I don't want to marry him, Theadosia. I scarcely know the duke." She heard the pleading in her voice but didn't care. She couldn't wed a virtual stranger. "I'm confident Bainbridge doesn't want this either."

For all she knew, he lamented his broken betrothal with Miss Brighton. Or, if he didn't, he'd not be eager to enter into a marriage of convenience when he'd just escaped an arranged marriage.

Jessica was no fool. She knew how womanizers of his ilk behaved: They married, beget an heir or two on their wives, then bustled their inconvenient spouses off to the country so the rogue could carry on, unhindered, with his string of mistresses and lovers.

"I'm truly sorry, but you must, Jessica. It's the only way to preserve his name and your reputation."

Rakehells don't have any honor.

"The nuptials were Bainbridge's suggestion," Theadosia went on, either unmindful of Jessica's mutinous scowl or choosing to ignore it. Likely the latter. "He is an honorable man and, from what Victor has told me, kind, too." She touched two fingertips to the bridge of her nose as if her head also pained her. "James intends to procure a special license on your behalf today, should it be required. I prefer the banns be put up, but that might not be possible."

Both notions rather galled.

Heavens, why not just hie off to Gretna Green? Do things up brown? Why, the only tidbit that might make this *on dit* juicier was if she were already increasing. *Oh God.* She could taste the bitterness of fresh bile in her mouth. People would likely believe she was pregnant, too.

Their brother, James, was a highly sought-after solicitor and, of late, a successful investor. A keener, more intelligent mind, Jessica had never encountered. Perhaps he might have an alternative solution.

Say, an extended holiday to France or Italy? For a decade. No, better make that two decades. Wouldn't do to rush home before *le beau monde's* exasperatingly long memory had faded.

"Victor, as well as the Dukes of Dandridge, Sheffield, and Pennington, are already spreading their own tattle," Theadosia revealed. "It's a rather good tale we concocted last night while you slept."

Jessica slanted an eyebrow up, skeptically. "Just what is this *tale*?"

Appearing a mite chagrined, her sister pressed her lips tight. She clasped and unclasped her hands before releasing a long sigh, her shoulders slumping.

"We're saying that Bainbridge recently became aware of Miss Brighton's affair with Brookmoore. He formally intended to break their betrothal on the grounds of infidelity. We're also spreading it about that the duke once confessed to Victor that, if he were a free man, he'd ask for your hand," she said, her voice slightly raspy. "We'll let people think they're clever and put two and two together."

Jessica shook her head and made a harsh movement in the air with her hands. "And you think anyone with a brain larger than a grape is going to believe that twaddledash?" She was forever mixing up her expressions, but right now, she didn't give a fig.

She fisted her hands, curled her toes, and clamped her teeth until they were in danger of cracking, so overwhelming was her fury.

Jessica resisted the impulse to thump the undeserving pillow again. But something—no, somebody—needed to be throttled. Make that two somebodies. "I wouldn't believe that fustian rubbish if I heard it. It sounds exactly like what it is. A monumental tarradiddle, confabulated to detract gossip. It won't work."

"The *haut ton* may not believe it, but given the rank of the peers insisting it's the truth, they won't dare imply otherwise." A note of satisfaction threaded Theadosia's voice. Apparently, she was learning just how advantageous it was to be a duchess.

It seemed everything had been decided while Jessica slept. Her life and future had been mapped out without a word of input or consent from her. A twinge of anger sliced through her.

Yet, in her core, she grudgingly acknowledged her sister spoke the truth. Her only hope of salvaging anything from this scandal was a prompt marriage. And marrying a duke, particularly the duke in question, was even better.

Miss Brighton and Brookmoore deserved one another. *God rot the wretches. May they be miserable every day of the rest of their despicable lives.*

"Brookmoore had better watch himself if he ever

dares to return to London. James or Victor might very well call him out." After tucking her handkerchief back into her bosom, Theadosia rose. She ran her palms over her tummy, a gentle smile framing her mouth.

She'd make an exceptional mother.

"If Bainbridge doesn't first," Jessica muttered sourly, convinced Crispin wouldn't turn a blind eye to the destruction of his honor and good name. Or for being compelled into the marriage trap.

Except James, Victor, or Crispin shouldn't have to jeopardize their lives on a field of honor with a soulless scoundrel such as Brookmoore.

"Come, my dear." Theadosia held out her hand. "Let's see you dressed to call upon your soon-to-be betrothed. I think you should wear something colorful. That new ice-blue gown and spencer will do. They fairly shout nobility to anyone who might see you. And we want to ensure the gossips don't find you lacking in any way."

Dear Theadosia. Surely she knew they would, in any event. Jessica would be dissected from toe to top. Every glance, every word, judged.

"But the duke is confined to his bed." If she met with Crispin today, this horror would become a reality. "I believe it would be wiser to wait until he's recovered."

That would give her time to contrive another solution.

"He's able to converse just fine, and he insisted your betrothal be made public today. We can't very well do that unless he asks you, now, can we?" Theadosia's false smile slipped a trifle.

Feeling mutinous and altogether cross, Jessica tossed the bedcovers back, snapping, "Don't be so very sure I'll agree to this farce."

7

Stifling a foul oath, Crispin sat perfectly still as his valet, Marsters, finished fussing over his hair, mindful not to bump the fresh bandage encircling his head.

"I don't think it's necessary to brush the top, Marsters, when this confines the rest of my hair." He waved two fingers at the linen strips. "I'll look ridiculous, despite your diligent efforts."

The valet spared him a brief look, his brows quirked in a mixture of annoyance and amusement. Though a foot shorter and at least two stones lighter, Marsters inevitably made him feel like a recalcitrant schoolboy.

"You're meeting with your betrothed, Your Grace," he explained with the patience one would address a gravely ill or mentally deficit individual.

Not betrothed *yet.* But before the day was out, Jessica Brentwood would be the future Duchess of Bainbridge. Pleasurable warmth swirled outward from Crispin's middle until it engulfed him like a cocoon.

"I cannot," Marsters went on, "in good conscience, permit you to leave this room unless you are at your very best."

Yes, someone might judge Marsters's skills deficient if Crispin's neckcloth wasn't tied just so. Or if a single speck of lint were spotted upon his fine-cloth burgundy coat. And heaven forbid if a smudge marred his footwear.

The stars might drop from the sky.

He gave one last flourishing swipe of the brush then stood back, inspecting Crispin from his head to his just-polished-to-a-high-gleam Hessians. With a satisfied nod, he declared, "You'll do."

"You're quite certain?" Crispin quipped, unable to keep the drollness from his tone.

Head cocked, Marsters *tutted* to himself. He stepped forward and flicked a minuscule speck of something invisible from Crispin's shoulder.

Thank God he'd spotted that; the world might've ended, had he not.

Why, Miss Jessica Brentwood might've torn from the room, yanking at her hair and screaming at the top of her lungs if she'd spied the speck.

Crispin would've shaken his head in amusement, just to fluster Marsters, but his skull still ached bloody awful. After all, it had been less than four and twenty hours since he'd been knocked from behind hard enough to require twelve stitches. An egg-sized lump protruded beneath the bandages.

It was almost enough to make him wonder if Brookmoore hadn't been intent on killing him, rather than rendering him incapacitated. Did the sod seriously think he could avoid repercussions for his actions? It made more sense to believe Brookmoore had taken leave of his faculties.

Or, perhaps, he was desperate. Desperate men did all manner of stupid things.

Nevertheless, Crispin would be damned if he'd propose to Jessica from his bed, like an invalid. Bad enough, he didn't have a ring for her. That could be remedied in short order, however.

Since he didn't know her gemstone preference, mayhap they'd make an outing of it. He'd determined to give her something unique. Something no one else had ever worn. A ring that would make her eyes sparkle with appreciation.

Naturally, there were dozens and dozens of majestic gems, parures, and other blinding and glittering baubles in the family safe. But Jessica warranted a betrothal ring that commemorated their union. He couldn't help but wonder how she'd reacted to the news of their disgrace and forthcoming nuptials. Crispin would do all within his power to ease her discomfit and any concerns.

Toward that end, he would meet his future duchess in the drawing room. Despite Marsters's fierce scowl and downturned mouth; his housekeeper, Mrs. Peedell's, *tsking* and issuing vexed and dire warnings that he would kill himself; and his majordomo,

Barlow's, elevated nose and loud sniffs of disapproval, he'd left his bed two hours ago.

There'd be no chastisements to his domestics for overstepping, for their actions were born out of affection and loyalty. In truth, he counted himself lucky to have them.

The long soak in the tub had helped a degree, as had the medicinal tea laced with herbs that Mrs. Peedell had threatened to pour down his throat while Marsters and Barlow held him unless he drank the bitter concoction. He'd far have preferred Scotch or cognac, but he'd been forbidden spirits until his concussion healed.

That was bloody inhumane torture.

All the while he readied himself for his meeting with Jessica, rage—acrid and lethal—simmered behind his ribs. A steady, bubbling fury.

No one, by God, *no one* conspired against him in the manner Brookmoore and Lilith had and didn't dearly pay for their perfidy. That he was forced to ask for Jessica's hand in marriage only magnified the insult.

Now, she'd never believe he'd yearned to marry her, to make her his. Before this debacle, he'd not been able to declare himself or ask permission to court her. Being betrothed did rather curb wooing another woman, even if the duke possessed a wicked reputation.

A reputation he'd methodically and diligently cultivated, hoping to dissuade the Brightons. A reputation built on falsehoods and fabrications. And although his carefully constructed facade had failed to convince the Brightons to void the betrothal contract, Society had been all too eager to accept the charade as absolute truth.

Nevertheless, he couldn't deny the prospect of marrying Jessica excited him.

What infuriated Crispin, and what he'd never be able to convince others of, was that she'd have been his choice had he been given one. He'd have courted her, wooed her, hoping that, in time, she'd come to care for him.

Nevertheless, due to the duplicity of others, the decision of whether to wed or not had been ripped from them.

A slightly evil grin tipped his mouth on one side.

How was Hammon Brighton dealing with his darling daughter's treachery?

Wouldn't Crispin like to be a fly in the room when Brighton learned of her duplicity. Her ruination, for she was every bit as disgraced as Jessica, if not more. And when her part in the fiasco wrought upon him and Jessica became known, not a door would remain open to her or her parents, no matter how deep and heavy their purses.

Only an absolute idiot bashed dukes over the head, stripped them naked, and arranged them for discovery with an equally nude, drugged female and hoped to escape unscathed. Hoped to escape his wrath.

Never having struck him as a female with particularly sharp intellect, Lilith probably hadn't even considered the ramifications for herself. He'd be bound, her only consideration had been how to discredit Crispin in order not to wed him. That she'd also injured an innocent, someone incapable of the degree of deceit and callousness she had shown, made her contemptible and unworthy of mercy.

He scratched his nose, considering the steps he'd take to assure appropriate justice was meted out.

It would be hers and Brookmoore's word against his and Jessica's, though. That might prove a trifle tricky, particularly since Radcliffe could be counted on to substantiate any tale his foul brother concocted.

If only there'd been a witness to Jessica entering the hothouse with Lilith. Better yet, someone who'd seen Brookmoore and Lilith undress him and Jessica, or him being struck upon the head. That was about as likely as snow in August.

Pink snow.

Hammon Brighton, the mule-headed mushroom, had refused for years to release Crispin from the contract. But now, Lilith had assured his freedom.

A half-snort, half-chuckle escaped him, causing Marsters to give him a dubious look before turning his attention back to the task at hand.

Perchance Crispin ought to thank Lilith for helping him snare the one woman he'd dreamed of making his own; rub a little salt in the wound, as it were. His grin grew wider at the thought. No court would uphold the betrothal contract now —neither a court of law nor the court of public opinion.

What was a little humiliation and discomfort to be rid of the chit once and for all? Well, a jot more than a little, but he was thick-skinned. But was Jessica? He'd found women tended to be much more sensitive about matters of this nature.

Victor had already bought up Radcliff's vowels on Crispin's behalf, but he wasn't done with Brookmoore and his brother. Not by half, by God. They'd only begun to feel the power of his wrath. By the time he'd finished with them, they'd never show their faces in London again. Maybe not even England.

Slowly rising, for sudden movement sent his head and his stomach swirling, he stood and waited for the room to stop wobbling. He shouldn't be up and about yet. He blamed his deuced pride. One did not propose while flat upon one's back in bed. Truth be told, he shouldn't have to propose under these circumstances at all, but little good it would do to voice that fact.

Lines of concern stamped Marsters's face, but he

wisely kept his apprehension to himself. "I'll just walk with you, Your Grace."

In other words, *I'll make sure you don't fall flat on your face and ruin my efforts to see you presented in the first stare of fashion.*

Crispin wouldn't dismiss his offer.

He might very well need an arm to lean on if his head didn't stop spinning. In truth, he also might cast up his accounts. Jaw clenched against the pain stabbing his brain, he managed to make the drawing room without disgracing himself. And with seven minutes to spare before the clock struck four, he sank onto the brocade sofa before the comfortably snapping fire.

He'd opted against meeting Jessica in his study. The atmosphere would be too formal and intimidating. Most likely, she was already apprehensive and embarrassed. As much as possible, he'd ease her discomfort. The truth was, the whole situation was deucedly awkward.

Last night, barely able to string one thought after another, he'd demanded the flustered women, who'd intruded upon him and Jessica in the conservatory, remain to lend the merest thread of respectability while he'd sent the gawping men for help. Namely, to locate Jessica's family and Westfall, as well as Dandridge, Sheffield, and Pennington and their duchesses.

Once her sister and his friends had arrived, he'd sent the first intruders on their way, in no uncertain terms. Sheffield stood guard outside the door, deterring additional inquisitive guests who'd made their way from the main house when word of the debacle had broken.

At that thought, he pressed his mouth into a harsh line. That had to have been something to witness. He could only imagine the *sotto voce* whispers, sly smiles, and waggling eyebrows.

Bainbridge and Jessica Brentwood are tangled together, naked as cherubs, in the hothouse.

The young duchesses, amid appalled whispers, had bundled the still-unconscious Jessica into her clothes as best they could, while the men gently assisted Crispin, peppering him with questions he could scarcely answer, half-unconscious himself.

Someone had sent for a physician, and Pennington

and Sutcliffe had accompanied him home. Once the physician had examined Crispin and he'd explained Brookmoore's and Miss Brighton's part in the scheme, he'd fallen into a restless slumber. Made more so by Mrs. Peedell, Marsters, or Barlow waking him every hour to ensure he hadn't cocked up his toes.

Not before vowing he'd wed Jessica at the earliest opportunity, however. Even in his befuddled state, he recognized that was their only recourse.

There was no help for it, as he'd told Sutcliffe, who whole-heartedly agreed with no small amount of relief as well.

Barlow rapped lightly before striding into the drawing room. "The Duke and Duchess of Sutcliffe and Miss Jessica Brentwood have arrived."

"Please show them in, and ask Mrs. Peedell for tea and refreshments." Careful not to jostle his head, Crispin shoved to his feet. A gentleman would never remain seated when a duchess entered the room. The stilted movement nearly caused his eyes to cross in pain, but teeth clamped tight, he'd donned a benign mask.

"At once, Your Grace." Head lowered, Barlow backed out, the epitome of a deferential servant. For the moment, at least.

Uncharacteristic and unexpected nerves rioted around in Crispin's gut. As thankful as he was to no longer be betrothed to Lilith, he'd not thought he'd ever be in a position of asking a woman to marry him to avoid a scandal.

Avoid a scandal?

Too bloody late for that.

But, as an influential duke, he could provide Jessica with a position of power. Duchesses were forgiven much. Not that the troublesome circumstances surrounding their discovery in the conservatory wouldn't keep viperish tongues wagging for a few weeks. Even when the truth came out—for he'd see it did—the havoc had been wrought.

And it was damning.

The *haut ton* was more willing to turn a blind eye to a duke's or duchess's imprudence than to those of lower ranks. He held no qualms about exploiting his position if it ensured buffering Jessica against maliciousness.

A few deep, steadying breaths later, in which the turmoil in his head abated a degree, Barlow ushered the Sutcliffes and Jessica inside the drawing room.

Crispin succeeded in remaining upright without gritting his teeth or feeling faint. "Thank you for coming." He spoke directly to Jessica.

She wore a stunning, pale-blue day gown, the shade a perfect enhancement for her fair hair and vibrant eyes. Slight plum-tinted shadows ringed those pretty eyes today, and her features appeared more pronounced in her oval face. To the unpracticed eye, she exuded poise, but the angle of her jaw, the slope of her shoulders, and her stiff spine bespoke untold tension.

"I hope you are recovering well, Your Grace." Her voice had always fascinated him. Low and lilting, it held none of the arrogant coolness so many women of station affected.

After meeting his gaze and offering a cordial, if somewhat hesitant smile, her attention shifted to inspecting the room. Or, at least, she made a pretense of doing so.

He imagined, given what she no doubt knew about how they'd been found last night, she wrestled with a great deal of chagrin. He caught her regarding him from the corner of her eye.

Inquisitiveness and speculation shone there.

"How are you feeling, Bainbridge?" Sutcliffe asked as they shook hands. "I didn't expect to see you up yet. Didn't the doctor restrict you to bed for a week?" He chuckled and brushed a finger across an eyebrow. "Though, if it were me, I'd likely be out of bed against the physician's orders too."

"Indeed, you would." The duchess came forward and offered Crispin her hand. "Thank you, Your Grace. I cannot express how indebted I am to you for what you did for my sister last evening. I'll be forever obligated to you."

Crispin counted himself extremely fortunate that not a single one of his friends or their wives had doubted his tale. Though the evidence indicated he and Jessica had been the victims of foul play, there were still those with suspicious minds who suggested he was somehow at fault.

His friends were not amongst them.

As for being at fault… He berated himself a hundred times over for not at once suspecting Brookmoore was up to mischief when they'd entered the conservatory and he'd seen Jessica. He'd never been a particular friend of Brookmoore, but he'd never have suspected the churl would act so dishonorably, either. The truth was, seeing her lying there had so alarmed him, he'd cast aside his usual caution.

Still, the Duchess of Sutcliffe wouldn't be so appreciative if she knew he'd looked his fill at Jessica's lush curves. But then, he'd had little recourse, positioned as they were, both incapable of rising without assistance.

Something that felt very much like a flush warmed his face. "I shan't lie and deny my head hurts like the devil himself is kicking the inside of my skull, and the stitches are tender. But the physician assures me I'll recover, in due time."

Jessica cut him an assessing glance, her gaze probing. Her concern seemed genuine. "I hope you do so swiftly."

Her contralto voice wrapped around him like warm silk and took root in his heart. Only this woman had ever affected him thus.

"Please, won't you have a seat and make yourselves comfortable?" Crispin gestured toward the sofa as he claimed an armchair. The women sank gracefully onto the broad, ivory- and mint-hued cushions, and Sutcliffe took possession of the other plush armchair.

Jessica met his eyes, hers uncertain and apologetic beneath fine, winged eyebrows. As she removed her gloves, she delicately cleared her throat. "Before anyone says anything, I have something I wish to say."

8

Going on the offensive, was she? Crispin rather liked Jessica's gumption. She'd never been retiring or simpering. She'd just been…Jessica. Sweet and kind and wholly desirable.

She gently laid the gloves on the sofa's arm. The Brentwoods had been quite impoverished, and although Sutcliffe had provided her with a new wardrobe, Crispin liked that she continued to take care of her possessions, lest they become ruined.

Surprise registering on their faces, her sister and brother-in-law exchanged befuddled glances before turning their attention to her.

"What is it, dearest?" the duchess asked. The

sisters were extremely close.

Jessica had gone to live with the Sutcliffes after her parents sailed to Australia under a shroud of disgrace. That was all she needed. More ignominy after her father's dishonesty had tainted the family name.

Drawing in a breath deep enough to expand her chest, she clasped her hands and tilted her dainty-but-determined, slightly impertinent chin. "I know why we've come here today. I want to make it known that such a gesture is not necessary. I shan't accept, in any event."

"Pardon?" Her sister sent a panicked glance to her husband.

Jessica's chin inched up a trifle more, and she met Crispin's gaze straight on. She was a plucky thing, by Jove.

"But, Jessica, we spoke of this." The duchess's concern for her sister was tangible. He'd seen her alarm last night. He saw the tears she'd shed upon spying her younger sister. Witnessed the sharp snap of anger jerking her eyebrows together and straightening her spine when she realized the May game that had been played upon Jessica.

She only wanted what was best for her sister and, like Crispin, acknowledged the most prudent of actions was a swift exchanging of vows.

Sutcliffe leaned forward, compassion etched upon his usually sardonic features. "Why don't we discuss the situation first, and then you can make a decision?"

He glanced at Crispin for confirmation, and he gave a slight nod, cognizant any abrupt movement might send his head bouncing across the floor as violently as a nut shaken in a tin. His soon-to-be bride might not appreciate the scene.

Barlow entered with the tea service. "Will there be anything else, Your Grace?"

"No. Thank you. Please close the door."

He appreciated the servants would likely listen at the keyhole, and he hadn't a doubt news of last night's debacle had already swept through the house, from the attic to the kitchen. In all likelihood, they also knew why Jessica was here and had already begun to assess their new mistress.

"May I impose upon you to pour, Miss Brentwood?" She might as well begin her role as his duchess.

A startled look whisked across her refined features before she schooled her emotions and dipped her chin in acquiescence. "Of course."

As always, her voice washed over him, at once soothing and arousing. He didn't let his imagination trot down the latter, more sensual path, or he'd be sporting a cockstand. That, he didn't want to have to explain to his future brother-in-law.

With the inherent grace he so admired about Jessica, she completed the task, and after everyone held a cup of tea and had selected an assortment of sandwiches and dainties, he cleared his throat. "Thank you for coming today. I shan't dally or mince words."

He slid Jessica a glance, but her focus remained fixed on her shoes. Or the carpet. Or perhaps it was the absolutely riveting turn of the table's leg.

"You needn't ask for my hand in marriage, Your Grace," she quietly said, without a hint of regret or subterfuge as she brought her gaze up to meet his.

Again, she reminded him of a marine-eyed kitten.

"It's noble of you if that's your intent," she conceded. "But I find, in truth, I have neither the temperament nor the inclination to become a duchess."

The room grew unnaturally silent, the Duchess of Sutcliffe casting her husband a panicked look, her teacup poised in midair. The exuberantly crackling fire and the clock's steady ticking filled the awkward space.

Turned down before he'd even proposed. This didn't bode well. Jessica must be convinced to change her mind, must see that marriage to him was the only solution.

Sutcliffe cleared his throat. "See here, Jessica. I'm your guardian in your father's absence, and I don't believe there's any other recourse. If there were, I'd not have brought you here today."

Well, thank you very much. Crispin speared Sutcliffe a dark glower.

Once she'd set her teacup aside, the duchess touched her sister's arm, concern shadowing her pretty face. "What's really going on, my dear? There's more to this than simple reluctance to wed a man you don't know well. I explained this morning how unfortunate the circumstances are. We"—she swept her hand in an arc to include Crispin and her husband—"fear for your future."

"Might I have a few moments alone with Miss Brentwood?" Crispin asked, his focus never straying from her.

The duchess darted him an astonished look before her features settled into a contemplative mien. She sent her husband a speaking glance. One that demanded he'd bloody well better acquiesce, and he nodded.

"It's rather unorthodox, but yes. I suppose you might," he slowly agreed, uncrossing his legs.

Jessica snorted indelicately, shaking her head as if they were silly children. "I cannot imagine a few moments alone would be any more objectionable than a half dozen people coming upon us lying naked and entwined together."

Clearing his throat, Sutcliffe shifted uncomfortably, and his wife blushed as she pressed a palm to the juncture of her collarbone.

Why did adults act all discomfited and constrained whenever anyone mentioned the words *naked* or *nude*?

At once, Crispin's mind flashed back to last night. Of Jessica's pearly-white, satiny body melded to his. Of her scintillating cloves and vanilla scent. It took every ounce of his will not to drop his attention to her breasts. He could still envision them in his mind: plump, creamy mounds with perfect rosebud-pink nipples.

Sutcliffe would run him through if he had any notion the dangerous path Crispin's thoughts had jogged down.

Despite her advancing pregnancy, the duchess angled agilely to her feet. At once, the men stood, and Crispin's head spun dizzily from rising too swiftly. "I should very much enjoy a stroll through your gardens, Bainbridge." She gave her husband a blinding smile. "Darling, shall we?" She took his arm for, *of course,* he didn't dare say otherwise.

"I know the way," Sutcliff allowed. "I'll permit you ten minutes."

"That's all I require," Crispin assured him.

The room remained unnaturally still after their departure. Jessica poured herself more tea and then, teapot in hand, inquired, "Do you care for any more, Your Grace?"

"No, and please call me Crispin. Or Cris. And I shall address you as Jessica. Unless you have another preference?"

A golden eyebrow flexed at his suggestion, but she didn't argue. "No. Unlike Theadosia, my name was never shortened. I cannot abide being called Jess or Jessie. What is it you wished to discuss with me that you couldn't say in front of my sister and Victor?"

She blew lightly on her hot tea, drawing his attention to her cupid's bow mouth. A shade between pink and cherry, her kissable lips all but begged for him to sample their sweetness.

Condemning propriety to a fusty corner, he took her sister's place beside her. If she hadn't been clutching the teacup like a miniature shield, he'd have taken her hand in his.

"Jessica, I believe you feel I've been pressed into asking for your hand against my will. That the circumstances of last night have necessitated it, and that is the only reason why I would marry you."

Both eyebrows shied up her forehead before she wrinkled her small nose.

"You shan't convince me otherwise, Your Grace. And I shan't marry a man for no other reason than he is obligated by duty and honor to offer for me because of the nefarious actions of others." She shifted her focus away, staring at the fire, unhappiness and melancholy shadowing her lovely face.

Ah, she was more overwrought than she'd let on. How could she not be?

That her concern was for him, and not herself, caused an indecipherable twinge behind his breastbone. For the truth of it was, he could choose to walk away and maintain his social standing.

Oh, there'd be chatter, of course. But a wealthy duke would never be permanently shunned, and women would still vie to become the next Duchess of Bainbridge.

She, on the other hand, had no future. Not a respectable one, if she didn't accept Crispin's offer.

He'd replace her despondency with laughter and gaiety if she'd only permit him. They could be happy together.

"As silly as it may seem to you, my sister, and brother-in-law, I'd rather suffer the snubbing and disgrace than enter into a compulsory union. The shame will fade eventually, replaced by other titillating *on dit*. But a marriage..." She shook her head, golden ribbons from the window's light shimmering in her blonde hair.

He reached to touch a flaxen curl but drew his hand back. Too bold, too soon. But, someday, he'd run his hands through those sunny curls, bury his face in their silkiness, and inhale Jessica's heady fragrance.

"Marriage is for a lifetime," she said. "And I cannot imagine a more dissatisfying scenario than to enter into what could very well be an incompatible union."

Making a sympathetic noise, he took the cup from her and set it aside. He did claim her hand then, running his thumb across the palm. "And what if I told you that I've held you in high esteem for quite some time? That only my betrothal to Miss Brighton kept me from proclaiming myself and asking for permission to pay my addresses?"

It was God's honest truth. And damn it all, if it didn't feel blessedly wonderful to declare himself finally.

Her luscious mouth went slack for a second, and she blinked her big blue-green eyes twice, appearing adorably birdlike in her astonishment. Her gaze plumbed Crispin's, solemn and penetrating, as if she sought something within the depths of his eyes.

An assurance? Affirmation that he spoke the truth?

Aye. That and perhaps more. Mayhap a desire, a hope that he felt something for her? He'd been her secret admirer for some time.

He'd confounded her. It rather stung his pride that she should be so shocked.

"In no way did you ever hint of such interest, in word or deed," she said, narrowing her eyes slightly, the silver flecks glinting with suspicion. "How am I to believe you now?"

He sensed her hesitation, her uncertainty. That it would make a difference to her if he wed her because he wanted to instead of out of obligation.

"I am a gentleman, Kitten. I could not speak of my interest while betrothed to another. I vow others have noted my attentiveness to you." He recalled the Duke of Pennington teasing him about his hang-dog expression as Crispin surreptitiously observed Jessica. "They've seen me covertly watching you."

Devil it. The confession made Crispin sound like a stalker.

"Watching me?" A scowl tweaked her eyebrows and framed her mouth. "Who saw you?"

Such distrust and suspicion.

If Jessica noticed the term of endearment, she'd chosen to ignore it. He hadn't meant to let it slip.

"Pennington. Sutcliffe. And others." He might as well admit it. There was no longer a reason to hide his fascination for her. He pressed her fingertips, wishing he might lift the slender fingers to his mouth. "I've attempted to have my betrothal contract canceled for some time. If you think about it, I often arranged to be present where you were. House parties, and the like."

He *had*, more fool him.

"Did you?" Her nose angled slightly higher. "I hadn't noticed."

Was that the truth, or was the vixen toying with him? He detected no subterfuge, but her comment was slightly too flippant.

"You do owe me an ice from Gunter's," she reminded. "Which I shall have before Season's end, mind you."

"Name the date, and it shall be done." He breathed a silent sigh of relief that she'd changed the subject.

Jessica pursed her pretty mouth before blurting, "Your betrothal didn't prevent you from numerous dalliances."

Good God. She wanted to discuss his lovers? *Past* lovers.

That, he would not do, out of respect for the few women who'd graced his bed and from a desire to protect her from what surely could only be painful and embarrassing disclosures.

Her color high and nostrils slightly flared, she

challenged him in that direct way he so admired.

"I heard of your exploits before I came to London, Your Grace. I'm not a woman who could look the other way." Sadness and resignation settled on her features. "You're not the sort to keep yourself only to your wife."

I could be. For Jessica, he had no doubt he could.

It did, however, rather rankle to be dismissed so readily. To be found wanting in her eyes.

She bent her pink mouth into an unrepentant smile, her eyes flashing with turquoise sparks. Lifting a graceful shoulder, she flippantly waved her hand. "I'm old-fashioned that way. Vicar's daughter, and all that. I'd expect fidelity, and I doubt you're capable of faithfulness."

Crispin wasn't sure whether to laugh or be offended. Life with her would certainly be an adventure.

Releasing Jessica's hand, he considered how to reply. She deserved transparency and honesty. He unthinkingly cupped the back of his head as he did when in thought, and a sharp breath hissed from between his clenched teeth.

Christ on the cross! He almost swore aloud. He'd forgotten about the bloody wound. He squeezed his eyes shut, clamped his teeth tighter, and held his breath, waiting for the stab of pain to pass.

As it eased, he opened his eyes.

"Crispin?" Sincere worry tinged her voice. "Are you quite all right?" At once, her features pleated into concern, and she laid a dainty hand atop his forearm. Her fingers were slender, but not overly long, the nails short and oval-shaped.

"Should I send for someone?" she asked, her fingers still resting on his forearm, further disrupting his equilibrium. Her innocent touch sent his libido racing. "Do you require pain medicines? Or should you lie down?" She made as if to rise, but he stayed her with a palm over her hand.

"No, I'm fine, Jessica. Truly." He wasn't, but they must work out the issue of their nuptials. He could rest later.

"I don't suppose you'd believe me if I told you the bulk of what you've heard was a ruse, fabricated to encourage Brighton to break the betrothal contract?" He leaned back, welcoming the sofa's support. He bussed his hand over his jaw. "I'd hoped if I were a bad enough scapegrace, he'd refuse to bind his only daughter to me."

Jessica's delicate eyebrows shied high onto her alabaster forehead. Her expression fairly shouted liar. Prevaricator. Charlatan.

When he laid it out like that, his plan sounded damned absurd, even to him.

No man with Brighton's social aspirations would object to something so trivial as a sordid reputation. *Or by-blows and mistresses.* In short, Crispin might've been a diseased debauchee, and Brighton would still insist the marriage take place.

"That was rather extreme, wasn't it?" Jessica toyed with her earring, considering him the whole while.

She appeared neither shocked or judgmental. No, if anything, he'd say she was mystified.

"You burden yourself with a much-tainted repute to escape marriage, Crispin? Such an albatross, obviously, would be problematic to overcome."

"Not marriage," he denied with the merest shake of his head.

"No?" Her probing gaze said she didn't believe him.

"I have no dislike of the institution itself. What I object to, most strongly, is matrimony to a woman I was pledged to as a child, to whom I have no warm regard whatsoever." He played his fingers upon his knee, realizing just how little he felt for Miss Brighton except scathing anger. "Besides, I was determined to see the engagement ended without a scandal," he admitted, crossing his ankles.

Her wry smile, hilarity in her aquamarine eyes, and the mocking angle of her winged, golden eyebrows spoke volumes. "Yes, well, that certainly worked out well, didn't it?"

She jested. *Minx.*

When was the last time he'd enjoyed a conversation this much? Even if the circumstances were, to say the least, trying as hell.

Two could play at teasing, though why they were

verbally parrying when they should be discussing the terms of their marriage, he couldn't quite define. He'd thought to take control of the situation, and Jessica had neatly turned the tables on him. Crispin would have to remember that in the future.

Despite having been outmaneuvered last night by Miss Brighton, Jessica was not easily manipulated. He rather liked that. Liked that she knew her own mind. Appreciated that she wasn't weepy and hysterical at her plight.

He angled his own eyebrows in feigned reproach. "Have *you* ever seen me with a woman on my arm? Has a particular lady's name *ever* been linked with mine?"

Crispin had been most diligent that neither of those occur.

His rake's reputation was built on inference and insinuation. Whispers and conjectures. Implication and allusion. It had been remarkably easy to create something out of nothing. There were always those at the ready to embellish a whisper. Add intimations and innuendos.

She slanted her head in an endearing fashion, indecision and doubt darkening her eyes to almost indigo. "Not a respectable woman, no. But there are, ah…" She blushed furiously but plowed onward, the brave darling. "There are *establishments* men might frequent. Women whose favors might be purchased."

Her cheeks glowed pink with chagrin.

Jesus and all the saints. How did a vicar's daughter know about bordellos and courtesans? He frequented neither, restricting his ventures to White's, Boodle's, and *Bon Chance*, none of which were gaming hells or brothels.

"Jessica, how can I convince you my exploits have been greatly exaggerated?" *Devil and damn.* His ploy to appear a philandering rakehell might very well make him irredeemable in her estimation.

And, unfortunately, it didn't matter what she thought of him. Though, of course, he'd much prefer she didn't dislike or disdain him, as he'd be her husband for many years, the good Lord willing.

For wed him, she must. In short order, too. She'd be the target of every whoremongering churl in

England if she didn't. Each thinking to sample charms they believed her eager to share. And some wouldn't wait for her permission; they'd force themselves upon her at the first opportunity.

Crispin would spare her that foul knowledge, if possible. No woman should ever know her good name had been reduced to such despicable depths.

She'd be dismayed to know there were already bets on the books at White's for who'd have her in his bed next. Marsters had shared that particularly unsavory tidbit with his usual stoic drollness while shaving Crispin. The valet had heard it from the underfootman, who'd heard it from his cousin, a waiter at White's.

Not even a full day had passed, and wagers were flying.

His stomach churned, and his head ached bloody awful, making him question the wisdom of leaving his sickbed. Pride, in his case, might literally go before a fall.

Plucking at her serviette, Jessica wrinkled her forehead. As if realizing she tortured the unfortunate cloth, she folded the square and set it aside.

He could practically hear the whirring of her brain as she considered what he'd said.

"Papa always said actions speak louder than words." She sighed and brushed a hand over the silky fabric of her skirt. A small sardonic smile skewed her soft mouth, and she slid him a glance from beneath her golden-tipped lashes. "This is a fine pickle, isn't it?"

"It is, indeed." It could be a most delicious pickle if she'd but agree to be his duchess.

She turned toward him then, her mouth quirked in the winsome way it did when she was contemplative. "Do you think Miss Brighton and Lord Brookmoore have married? Theadosia said everyone believes they've eloped, after…uhm, what they did to us."

Crispin gave a casual shrug. He didn't give a snap about either of them except that they be held accountable for their actions. "I cannot say, but that seems to have been their plan. No one knows for certain, of course."

Sutcliffe had sent a rider after them to report on their intentions, but to Crispin's knowledge, the man hadn't returned yet. Brookmoore and Miss Brighton might've evaded the man, too. Brookmoore was cunning. A scurrilous lout. He'd likely been bedding Miss Brighton for some time. He *was* precisely the sort to steal a maiden's virtue. She could count herself fortunate he'd been gentlemanly enough to wed her.

He'd left bastards in the wombs of many a woman. A responsible fellow made sure not to impregnate his partners. Brookmoore, by no stretch of the imagination, fit that category.

Crispin speared a glance at the spotless tall windows illuminating one side of the drawing room. The day had darkened somewhat, and a breeze ruffled the meticulously groomed shrubberies. Sutcliffe was most probably on his way back with his wife.

"Your sister and brother-in-law will return soon, Jessica. They'll expect you to have accepted my proposal."

She cradled her chin between her forefinger and thumb, head tilted to the side as she observed him. A spark of mischief gleamed in her eyes. Even now, she remained light-hearted and impish, when both of their futures hung in the balance.

"Ah, but then you haven't proposed, Your Grace, have you?"

9

Why in heaven's name had Jessica jested about Crispin's proposal?

The words had poured from her mouth of their own dashed accord. She'd meant what she said about not accepting his offer, however. Meant she'd somehow shoulder the cuts and snubs. Endure the doors slammed in her face. Bear the whispers and snide comments. Learn to accept the isolation and boredom ostracism brought.

It did bring her a smaller degree of satisfaction that Miss Brighton—possibly Viscountess Brookmoore, by now—would also bear a degree of rejection. Not, naturally, to the extent Jessica would. A vicar's daughter did not measure up to a viscountess—even a devious, deplorable, conniving one.

No wonder Crispin had no desire to wed the girl.

When he'd admitted he'd been trying to break his betrothal contract for some time, a little bell had pealed. She wasn't precisely certain what kind of signal it was—a warning or one to grab her attention?

Why would a man who'd been intent on avoiding marriage with one woman readily agree to wed another, especially one tarnished by scandal? Even if he was the other party contributing to her disgrace.

A man of Crispin's caliber, a philanderer, wouldn't jump straight from the pot directly into the fire. He'd celebrate his escape from the parson's mousetrap, wouldn't he? Sow more wild oats? Enjoy his narrow escape?

Nonetheless, his tone held a degree of sincerity Jessica couldn't readily dismiss. It shone in his compelling, smoky eyes, which drew her to him on a level she didn't understand but yearned to explore.

Even his scent—sandalwood, shaving lather, and starched linen—and the permeating heat of his body, mere inches from hers, beckoned. Enticed. Seduced.

And though she was inexperienced in such things, she believed he felt it, too. His focus kept dipping to her mouth, and several times, it appeared as if he would touch her then thought better of it.

Was she so gullible, so desirous of his attention, that she wished it so? Was she simply another female with whom to satiate his lust? That unsolicited thought made her ridiculously despondent.

She'd hoped he was as attracted to her as she was to him. Not wishing to be another notch upon his bedpost, metaphorically speaking, she'd fought that fascination for months, truth to tell. Some might argue she was easily deceived.

Miss Brighton was the perfect example of that.

No, by juniper. Jessica pulled her lips tight. She wouldn't blame herself for that treachery. There'd been no reason to mistrust the innocent-faced girl. It just went to show that first impressions could be most deceiving. She'd always looked for the good in people and wasn't adept at reading body language or eyes.

"Well, then, I'd best go about it properly, hadn't

I?" Crispin slid to the floor before her knees, abruptly dragging her back to the present.

She drew in a sharp breath, afraid he'd cause himself further injury. "You don't have to do that, for pity's sake." She speared the bandage circling his head a hard look. "Please do rise. I shall not be responsible for further injury to your person."

He was in pain. A lot of pain.

Fine white lines bracketed his mouth, and discomfort cinched the corners of his arresting, silvery eyes. But it was the dullness in their depths that revealed how much he suffered from his concussion.

He truly ought to be abed. Jessica would feel wretched if he didn't recuperate quickly because of some inane moral code that said he must propose upon one knee.

"I was but jesting, Crispin. I've already told you my decision." When had she started addressing him by his given name? It had seemed so natural; she'd slipped into doing so without thought.

He gave her one of his bone-melting smiles, and she was thankful her bum was planted firmly on a cushion, for her knees surely would've gone weak. Her ridiculous heart pattered unevenly, and something akin to giddy anticipation made her hot then cold in turn.

Bah, what a ninny.

Rakehells did this. Made each woman feel like she, alone, was precious and cherished. That they had no eyes for another. How Jessica wanted that to be true. She'd agree to marry him in a trice if it were.

On one knee, he took her hands in his. She couldn't help but notice the way the fabric stretched tautly over his indecently muscled thigh. He was a deuced fine specimen of manhood.

Good Lord. What would Papa say if he knew I curse in my head? Sometimes aloud, too.

She trailed her gaze over Crispin. His undeniable physical attributes had never been a cause for argument. In that, he was nearly incomparable. It was his character that lacked polish and morality.

He cradled her fingers in his warm palms, the gesture at once tender and enticing. "Jessica, I would be incredibly honored if you'd consent to become my wife."

"*Incredibly,* Your Grace? Isn't that doing it up a bit brown?" She spread her fingers, not at all surprised when he linked his with hers. "I'm not exactly a brilliant catch."

Not a blueblood, but a woman with a reputation besmirched beyond repair.

His hawkish eyebrows swooped together. "You're supposed to either accept or decline, Kitten, not critique the proposal. And I shall decide if you are a brilliant catch. And you most assuredly are."

"Oh, do pardon me. I'm just finding it somewhat difficult to take this quite as serious as I should, I suppose. Which, come to think of it, is rather peculiar, given the situation is most dreadful."

At his loud snort and wry look, laughter bubbled up her throat.

His eyebrows grew impossibly tauter.

"Not that your proposing is dreadful, I don't mean." She extracted her fingers—it was impossible to think straight with his thumb caressing her—and folded her hands atop her ice-blue gown. "Though I suppose it is, in a way, since it's not a proposal born of love. But I referred to last night's incident." She drew in a long breath and, eyes closed, slowly released it until her lungs were empty.

"Forgive me, Crispin. I'm babbling. I do so when I'm nervous."

She used to become tongue-tied and couldn't speak at all.

Which was worse?

"And I make you nervous?" His voice came out a silky purr, and her tummy turned over.

He knew he did. *Wretched man.*

She was no match for him when he decided to be charming and seductive. Was any woman?

"How can you not, Your Grace?"

Jessica shut her eyes for a blink but promptly envisioned them sprawled together, bare limbs entwined upon the divan. No one had explained precisely what that had entailed, and her imagination produced a most naughty image.

She popped her eyes back open and said in a rush, "I keep recalling we were found naked together. You, however, were awake, and I was not." She gave him a sideways glance. "I suppose you, um…saw me?"

Good God Almighty.

Jessica hadn't meant to blurt any of that. Yes, the question had been on the tip of her tongue since arriving, but she wrongly believed she'd tamed the dratted urge. She should only feel mortification and distress, not this unrelenting curiosity.

Had Crispin liked what he'd seen? Why should she care?

The darkening of his eyes to onyx and the dilating of his pupils revealed the astounding truth. His lazy gaze slipped to her bosom before gravitating upward to meet her eyes.

It felt as if he could see through her garments to the pale flesh below. As if he'd caressed that tender skin. She should be outraged and offended, but those most assuredly were not the feelings firing through her, causing weird tremors in unmentionable places.

And then he answered, leaning near, his breath feathering her cheek. A gentleman wouldn't have done so. "Indeed." Rich. Husky. Wicked. And tempting as sin.

She'd need to pray an extra hour tonight that God might forgive her for the lustful thoughts and feelings.

His lips moved near her ear. "From what I observed through my blurry vision, Jessica, you were *exquisite*."

Her breath caught and held.

Exquisite. Crispin finds me exquisite.

He's a rogue. Her sensible, moral, vicar's daughter self reprimanded.

All *roués* whisper such lovely nonsense. *Don't they?*

And now she'd gone and done the most humiliating of things: reminded him of their nudity. Of the reason she was here, and why he now suffered a fractured skull. Of the impossible situation they found themselves amidst.

"Incomparable," he purred silkily. Sincerely. Honestly. And the merest bit raspy.

"Oh." That was all she could achieve. One unimaginative syllable.

Oh, I'm delighted you liked what you saw? *Oh*, I should be swooning from mortification, but I'm not.

Oh, precisely, what *did* you see? How long did you stare?

Had he *touched* her?

Would he now?

Because Jessica very much wanted Crispin to. To kiss her. To wrap those strapping, powerful arms about her, and let her decide if the rumors about him lived up to the reputation. God, she certainly hoped they did.

Wicked. Wicked. *Wicked.*

A weak, mortified moan did escape her then.

A rough sound rumbling deep in his throat, Crispin wrapped a hand around the back of her head and pulled her to him. His mouth descended, fastening on her lips in a wit-scattering, pulse-stuttering kiss. She went perfectly still for a few heartbeats before the tender pressure had her opening to his probing.

"So sweet," he murmured. "I knew you'd taste of raspberries and honey."

He had? He'd wondered how her mouth tasted?

She parted her lips, and he slipped his tongue inside, brushing it across her teeth, then finding hers and parring seductively. Tantalizingly. Skillfully. God help her; she nearly incinerated on the spot.

He tasted of tea and mint.

Sensation flitted across her every nerve. *Closer. Yes, closer.* She must move closer to Crispin. She scooted to the end of the sofa and placed her hands flat, fingers spread, on his wonderfully sinewy, broad shoulders.

His muscles bunched and flexed beneath her palms, all rounded hardness and exciting virile maleness.

The kiss went on and on *and on*. Each moment more delicious and wondrous than the last. Each more sizzling. Satisfying yet oddly unfulfilling.

The passion dragged her under, encompassing, chasing away any thoughts of resisting or remorse. She *wanted* this. Had wanted it for so very, very long. Only she hadn't known it until his mouth took hers.

Her body felt hot and hungry in a way she couldn't understand, let alone explain.

"*Ahem.*" A slightly amused, somewhat censorious male cleared his throat and had her issuing a startled squeak and leaping backward as if singed.

Jessica *had* been seared. Branded. Burned by a desire so scorching, she'd nearly become a conflagration. No one had ever said passion could be like that.

"I do hope that means you've accepted Bainbridge's marriage proposal, Jessica," Victor said, not quite able to snuff the gleam of warning in the stern gaze he leveled on Crispin. "Else, I'll be compelled to demand satisfaction with pistols at dawn. It would be most unfair, given his current ill health."

"Don't be absurd, Victor," Theadosia interjected, swatting his arm, not quite playfully. "You're no more challenging Bainbridge to a duel than I am. Do you forget you are to be a father in a short time? I am not raising this child without its father." Though she bantered, there was a steely edge to her words. "It's only natural for a betrothed couple to share a kiss."

Jessica's sister had no intention of permitting her husband to risk his life over something as foolish as a kiss. But neither did she intend to ignore what the kiss implied.

Jessica and Crispin would wed.

Cheeks burning at being caught in another

compromising situation, though this one was far less scandalous and of her own making, she summoned her composure, and Crispin stood, quite nimbly for a man battling acute pain.

Flicking those long fingers of his at her, his gold signet ring with its knight's helmet and trio of battle axes glinted on his little finger with the casual movement. "I haven't received an answer yet."

At the dark look Victor stabbed him, Jessica quickly stood as well and shook out her skirts. "Yes. Yes, I agree to the union."

A trio of eyes swept to her. Relief and a degree of surprise in her sister's and Victor's gazes. A sensual, seductive promise simmering in Crispin's.

Another wave of awareness flooded her, heat swelling from her waist, over her bosoms, up her neck, and clear to her hairline. She swiftly averted her gaze, lest he see the answering spark that surely must shine in her own eyes.

She wasn't exactly sure at which point she'd made the decision. Before or after that breath-taking kiss? *Lord, but the man knew how to kiss.* Her mouth still throbbed from the delicious onslaught, and she was sure her lips were red and swollen.

"But," Jessica forced her attention back to them, disregarding the flush skittering over her when Crispin's hooded gaze settled upon her. "I want to wait until Crispin's concussion has fully healed. The gossip will be dreadful enough without rumors that he wasn't in his right mind when he proposed and we wed." She sliced him a glance. "I know you'd prefer we marry straightaway, but I must insist on the reading of the banns for three weeks. And no public announcement of the forthcoming nuptials until then."

"You have a valid point." Victor slowly nodded. "I hadn't considered that."

Crispin looked none too pleased, but after pulling on his ear, he also nodded. "I'll wait for three weeks. Not a day more. I fear we cannot delay longer than that."

They couldn't afford to wait *that* long. But three weeks gave her a little more time to become acquainted with him. To change her mind if she decided she couldn't go through with it.

Jessica gathered her gloves. "I would ask one thing of you, Your Grace."

10

"Crispin," he corrected. "We are affianced, after all." Taking Jessica's small hand in his much larger one, Crispin smiled that dashing smile that made her thoughts scatter like snowflakes in a blizzard. "I shall endeavor to make it come to pass, my dear."

My dear? Was he laying it on thick for Theadosia's and Victor's sakes? No need. Those two were prudent if naught else. They knew full well this was a marriage of convenience. Actually, more of a marriage of inconvenience, but a necessity, nevertheless.

"I want my pet chickens moved to your country estate."

She drew on a glove, refusing to be embarrassed at her attachment to her chickens. She'd very much like to ask for a puppy or two, a kitten or three, a horse of her own, and a donkey. Maybe even a pig and a sheep. Geese. Ducks. Goats. Best not to push her luck so soon, however.

Crispin might well change his mind when he realized his duchess intended to assemble a menagerie. Not exotic animals. No, they should remain free. But an assortment of domesticated ones would be lovely.

Theadosia giggled and covered her mouth with her hand.

Looking nonplussed, Victor drolly muttered, "Thank God. I should warn you, Bainbridge. She puts crocheted jumpers on the things."

At Crispin's incredulous look, Jessica squared her shoulders. "They become chilled, particularly when molting. I've had Lady Featherston, Countess Chirpsalot, Baroness Beaksworth, Princess Poultry, and Queen Cluckingham since they hatched. They think me their mother."

"They do," Theadosia said between laughs. "They

follow Jessica everywhere. And the minute those hens hear her voice, they come running, squawking away. It's something to behold when they're wearing their jumpers."

Crispin pressed his lips to the knuckles of her bare hand. "By all means. Bring the brood. Shall I have a special coop built for them? Do they prefer one story or two? Perhaps cozy, satin-lined nesting boxes? China dishes from whence to eat?" He chuckled, his eyes alight with mirth.

"Make fun all you like, but they love me, and I love them." Yes, it was odd. But she adored animals. Chickens were the singular pets Papa allowed her, and only because they produced eggs.

"You may have as many chickens or other fowl as you like, Jessica." Crispin turned to Victor. "We are in agreement, then? The ceremony will be in three weeks? The Monday after the last reading of the banns?"

Victor looked to Jessica for affirmation, and she dipped her chin. "*If* the doctor agrees you're well enough."

What was the recovery period for a concussion?

Barlow cleared his throat as he stepped into the drawing room, holding a salver with a card atop it. "I beg your pardon, Your Grace. Mr. Hammon Brighton insists that he must speak with you at once. I told him you were otherwise engaged, but he was most insistent."

He turned to Victor. "This also arrived for you, Your Grace."

If the servant found anything unusual about delivering correspondence to someone other than his employer, he in no way revealed his astonishment.

Barlow passed a letter to Victor, who promptly broke the seal and read the contents. His mouth pulled into a grim line before he refolded the missive and tucked it into his pocket.

How peculiar. Why would Victor have post delivered here?

Before she could ask, a rotund man wearing a garish, bright-blue jacket and orange-and-yellow striped waistcoat shoved past the butler. Face flushed and his sparse red hair standing on end as if he'd repeatedly plowed his hands through its scraggly lengths, Mr. Brighton drew up short upon spying Jessica, her sister, and Victor.

Eyes narrowed to hostile slits, he stomped toward Jessica, pointing accusingly. "*You!*"

At his visceral animosity, she shrank back, thankful for Crispin's arm protectively snaking around her waist.

"I know who *you* are," Brighton snarled, revealing slightly uneven, yellowed teeth. "You're the strumpet everyone's been talking about. The lightskirt bent on stealing my daughter's betrothed."

"I beg your pardon?" Jessica bristled, curling her fingers, ready to scratch his eyes out for calling her a whore. "How dare you?"

"Stay calm, Kitten." Crispin spread his fingers at her waist and gave a little pulse of pressure while whispering in her ear. He leveled Brighton a frosty glare. "You overstep, Brighton."

Such icy contempt weighted each word that Jessica shuddered. Crispin wasn't a man to cross, and she was grateful they were not on opposing sides.

Theadosia's glare eviscerated the man, and she swept her furious gaze about the room as if looking for something with which she might skewer him. "You are beyond the pale, sir."

"I shan't have it. Do you hear me?" So angry his ears glowed red, Brighton spun to face Crispin. "This is just another stunt to try to avoid marrying my daughter. It won't work either, *Your Grace*."

Why would any father who claimed any affection for his daughter insist she wed a man she obviously loathed?

Smirking, Brighton shook his head, causing the sparse hairs atop to sway like giant orangey feelers. *Is orangey a word?* "I'll see you in court if you try to break the betrothal contract. And I'll not hesitate to drag this shameless harlot's name through the shite."

"Sir! You forget yourself." Theadosia raked her gaze over him in much the same way one would scrape manure from one's shoe.

"Every gossip rag and newssheet will be eager to print the tales I feed them about her," Brighton crowed, confident he had the upper hand.

Did he?

Much like raptors, gossips hovered about, ready to swoop in and attack anything weaker than themselves. And blackguards such as Brighton possessed no integrity. A tiny frisson of fright tip-toed across her shoulders, and she wrapped her hands about her waist in a protective gesture.

"Not if they want to remain in business, they won't." Crispin drawled with commendable calm but wintery finality.

Brighton leaned in, going toe to toe with him. "Watch me. I already have men willing to swear they've bedded the tart."

Bloody cur! Jessica made a choking sound as she clamped her teeth against several other unsavory oaths throttling up her throat. Shaken by the rage thrumming through her, she dug her fingernails into her palms.

"No doubt paid handsomely by you to say so," Crispin bit out, each word razor sharp.

"Prove it," Brighton sneered, folding his arms, his features smug. He bloody well thought he had them, the cur.

Theadosia gasped. Her appalled attention swung to Jessica then bounced right back to Brighton. “You’re a monster.”

“My God,” Jessica whispered, slanting into Crispin. As if things weren’t already abysmal, this villain was prepared to lie to blacken her name further.

“Now, see here.” Victor took up a position beside Crispin, his features taut with indignation. “You’ve gone beyond the mark, besmirching Miss Brentwood’s good name when it was *your* daughter who drugged her. And her lover who bashed Bainbridge on his head.”

Lover? Just how had Victor come by that morsel?

“Lies. All lies, I tell you—every foul, libelous word. Lilith told me *everything,* not more than an hour ago,” Brighton spluttered, shifting his muddy-brown glare between the three of them.

“Lilith?” A chill of trepidation slithered down Jessica’s spine. “But…she eloped with Lord Brookmoore last night.” She cast Crispin a questioning glance. Hadn’t they eloped? Had someone twisted the facts there, too? Or carelessly failed to learn the truth?

"She did no such thing." Brighton drew a handkerchief from his pocket and mopped his damp forehead. "More of your slanderous lies, wench."

Crispin went rigid, yet he kept his arm about her. It was an anchor, holding her steady in this emotional tempest. "Yes, she did. But Brookmoore threw her over, didn't he? Did he learn she wouldn't inherit a dime if she wed without your consent?"

Brighton blanched but still puffed out his chest. He looked like an oversized, brightly-plumed pigeon. "Are you casting slurs on my daughter's good name, Bainbridge?"

"No, but *I* am, Brighton." Victor raked a fuming glance over the sweaty little man, and his upper lip hitched in contempt. "I have it from a knowledgeable source your daughter did, in fact, enter a coach with Brookmoore. That said, coach had valises stashed inside, and that it did, indeed, make straight for the Scottish border." He patted his coat pocket where the letter lay.

Ah, so that was what that was all about.

"They stopped at the Cat and Crock Lodging

House *overnight*," Victor went on. "They shared a chamber and were overheard quarreling in the common room the next morning."

Jessica couldn't help but admire the speed at which her brother-in-law had seen Brookmoore and Miss Brighton pursued. Nor fail to appreciate his defense of her. Or Crispin's, either.

Victor cut Crispin a steady gaze and gave a sharp nod before pointing a scathing scowl at Brighton. "Your daughter did indeed reveal to Brookmoore that she'd be cut off without a cent for eloping. Poor chit fancies herself in love with the bugger."

If Miss Brighton hadn't been so conniving and devious, Jessica might've felt a twinge of pity for her.

"I'm sure Brookmoore vowed everlasting love," Victor drawled, sarcastically. "Until he realized he'd be saddled with a wife but without a marriage settlement. He, being the gallant gentleman that he is, acquired a mount and deserted her, leaving your daughter to return to London on her own. Which, I presume, she promptly did and fed you the cock-and-bull story she contrived along the way."

"That romance didn't last long," Theadosia remarked dryly, with perhaps the merest hint of gratification in her tone.

Brighton directed his scornful stare at Crispin's arm around Jessica's waist. "I don't care how many *loose* women you entertain before or after your marriage to my daughter. But marry her, *you* will."

"I think not," Crispin denied, a wry smile quirking his mouth as his welcoming heat burned into Jessica's side. The pleasant aromas of sandalwood, soap, and starch floated past her nostrils.

"Your daughter dissolved our betrothal when she arranged to have Miss Brentwood and me incapacitated and then absconded with Brookmoore." He crooked a superior eyebrow over merciless slate-dark eyes, his disdain palpable. "Do you comprehend the seriousness of the charges they face for attacking a duke?"

Brighton's fleshy, bewhiskered jowls worked as he clenched and unclenched his hands.

Scorn and anger emphasizing his angular, clean-shaven features, Crispin leaned over, intimidating the shorter man, who had the good sense to step back a pace. "I confess to being most grateful to Miss Brighton." He skewed his mouth sideways.

Casting him an astonished glance, Jessica tried to discern if he was serious. How could he possibly be grateful to the chit?

Bold as brass and in front of all, he gave her a devilish wink, and her tummy turned over in giddy excitement.

Gathering her hand in his, he brought it close to his chest, the gesture almost reverent. "Now, I am free to marry a woman of my choosing. Miss Brentwood has granted me the highest honor possible and agreed to become my wife. You, Brighton, can deal with your wayward daughter any way you see fit. But know this: If you do anything to disparage my future duchess, I. *Shall.* Destroy. You."

Moisture beading his forehead and upper lip, Brighton blanched, swallowing audibly while tearing at his neckcloth.

Crispin jerked his chin toward the door. "Now, leave my house, and never darken my doorstep again."

"I shall see you in court, then." Brighton stomped to the doorway. He looked over his shoulder, spearing Jessica with a loathing-filled glare before swinging his wrathful focus to Crispin. "Lilith carries your child."

11

Jessica stared blankly at the page of the novel in her lap, a new Gothic romance Nicolette Twistleton had sent over the morning after the *incident.* Far better to be busy and concentrating on something—*anything*—but the debacle on everyone's lips. Or Mr. Brighton's last vile, world-tilting accusation.

Was Lilith Brighton truly with child? Was the babe Crispin's?

Her stomach sank and clenched as it always did when she entertained the possibility. It left a hollow, sick feeling in her belly. She didn't want to believe the ugly accusation. Found it almost impossible to accept.

But his reputation.

Crispin had vowed his romantic escapades were exaggerated. Claimed he'd created a false persona with the intent of off-putting his betrothed. Twisting her mouth to the side, she furrowed her forehead into a scowl, directed at the unread words on the page.

Jessica wanted to believe him. Needed to believe him. *Had* believed him. For if the claim was valid, what was she to do?

Her tummy pitched sickeningly again.

In truth, Crispin and Lilith assuredly wouldn't have been the first couple to have anticipated their vows and consummated the union prematurely. Still torturing the edges of the poor book, she worried her lower lip.

Yet that didn't make sense.

Why would Miss Brighton have Crispin knocked over the head, then? Why arrange for Jessica to be caught and disgraced with him? Why elope with the viscount? It was much more likely Lord Brookmoore had impregnated the daft chit then, as Victor suggested, abandoned her.

Afterward, the wily wench had thought to entrap

Crispin. Oh, how Jessica longed for five minutes with the devious snake. She'd give Lilith Brighton a tongue lashing she'd not soon forget.

Bah! How many times had those same musings circled each other in her brain, like a dog chasing its tail? Why, she'd almost made herself dizzy. And that was why she did her utmost to keep her mind occupied. Yet, she hadn't advanced beyond the first chapter since the day Crispin had proposed.

Pinching her mouth tighter, she uncrossed her legs, stretched out before her on the rather hard settee. She wiggled her toes to ease the slight cramping of her muscles from having remained in the same position for too long.

Crispin had attended the Christmastide house party hosted by her sister and brother-in-law. Jessica had seen him at several gatherings in the ensuing months since, including the musical at the Twistletons' and tea and garden party at Theadosia's, where he'd lost the match of Pall Mall to her.

Not privy to his comings and goings, she had no way of knowing if he'd ventured to London regularly.

Town was but a four-hour journey on horseback. But to her knowledge—and Victor believed it true as well—Crispin had only just arrived in London with the rest of his cohorts in time for the start of Parliament.

As he was a close associate of Crispin's, Victor would know, wouldn't he?

She permitted a tiny smile of relief to curve her mouth and the tension knotting her shoulders and neck to relax a trifle. Victor was an excellent judge of character.

During the day, Jessica fared well enough. But at night, as she lay in her too-big bed when all was quiet except for the peculiar noises a sleeping house made, and she attempted to sleep, her mind replayed the dreadful scene in Crispin's drawing room.

With his incessant, unpleasant monologue, Mr. Brighton had been positively beastly, calling her a whore.

What was more, her deuced overly-creative imagination made a remarkable effort to fill in the lurid details she'd been oblivious to in her drug-induced slumber that night of the ball. Small mercy, that. She didn't want to know everything that had transpired. What she did know proved distressing enough.

How could Crispin stand to face the people who'd come upon them? Her instinct was to run and hide. His, she'd venture, was to confront and demand truth. Ducal airs, and all that.

What was it about aristocrats that made people bow and scrape before them? Those same sycophants wouldn't give her the time of day.

When that horrible night wasn't haunting her ruminations, or the humiliation of the snubs she'd already received from several denizens, genuine worry for Crispin smothered her.

Once Brighton had departed, he'd nearly collapsed. She'd vowed to herself, right then and there, she'd not discuss any of this ugliness until he was much improved. She'd keep her worries to herself.

He'd written daily, reporting on his tactics, when he should've been resting and concentrating on recovering. It could not be good for his health to deal with Brighton, the rumors, the authorities, and the rest of the odiousness that now enshrouded both of them.

That was how she thought of their situation. *Odious. Ugly. Vile. Loathsome.*

The situation continued to deteriorate, and honestly, she hated the helplessness she felt. Despised feeling powerless to rectify the wrong done to her and Crispin. She'd agreed to wed him because, if nothing else, she was pragmatic.

A woman in her precarious position had few—*very few*—respectable options. In truth, she didn't relish hieing off to some fusty corner of England or Scotland. To live in obscurity for the remainder of her days, kept company by a few cats and chickens. Maybe a goat and a donkey as well. And a darling puppy.

After all, it was her fondness for puppies that had landed her in this mess. She might as well benefit from it in some small measure. Plus, marriage to a man who could kiss her breathless and turn her bones to custard wouldn't be so awful. She'd secretly admired Crispin, never once considering she might catch his attention.

If his sizzling kisses were any indication, he wanted her just as madly, but his letters conveyed none of the passion he'd introduced Jessica to that day.

She hadn't known how to respond to his terse, fact-filled correspondences. It was as if he briefed a court on proceedings rather than penned missives to his betrothed. How odd to think of him as such. Except, he'd signed the letters, "Ever yours, affectionately," followed by a flourishing *C*.

Ever yours? Affectionately?

The kind of warm regard one held for a long-time acquaintance? Or the tender care or fondness reserved for a beloved sister? Possibly—that was what she fervently hoped—a stronger emotion?

The man was an enigma. A puzzle she couldn't quite piece together. These past months, she'd caught glimpses of who she believed Crispin was, and then he'd say or do something she hadn't expected, and the image she'd built of him in her mind had to be reconstructed all over again. He was far more complex than a simple rakehell. He hid a noble side, and she found herself admiring him more than she ought.

With a sigh, Jessica brought her gaze up to the window and idly fingered the page edges, the movement strangely soothing. An ebony-headed coal tit flitted from branch to branch in the dogwood tree outside the library window. Cocking its head, the little bird scampered along, dipping and bowing, singing all the while.

She adored birds, particularly songbirds. An abundance of coal tits populated Colechester, so she was quite familiar with the sweet, little things. Looking closer, she spied another coal tit bearing slightly more muted plumage.

Ah, he was showing off, the wee gallant gentleman.

Were they already mates? Or was he trying to win her favor?

Even as Jessica contemplated the thought, the female gave what could only be called a flirtatious dip of her beak and suggestive flick of her tail before flying off. At once, the male pursued her.

Oh, to be like those birds. How much simpler their mating habits were than humans.

Hushed feminine voices in the corridor announced she was about to be interrupted. Jessica hadn't even swung her feet to the floor when Ophelia Breckensole,

Nicolette Twistleton, and Rayne Wellbrook sailed into the chamber. Each resembled a spring blossom in their colorful gowns.

"Ophelia? Nicolette? Rayne?" She shoved to her feet, delighted to see them and simultaneously concerned at the risk they'd taken. *Good Lord.* They'd be ruined if anyone knew they'd called upon her. She was soiled goods, and they chanced degradation by associating with her. "Surely, you know you shouldn't be here."

"Darling, we could stay away no longer." Ophelia enfolded her into her soft embrace, holding her in a fierce hug. She drew back, and after bussing Jessica's cheek, she examined her features. "I've been so very worried about you. How are you managing, dearest?"

Her hazel gaze overly bright, Ophelia blinked rapidly, valiantly fighting the moisture pooling in her eyes.

"Of course Jessica's beside herself, but she's still holding her head up, as she well should," Nicolette declared, swooping in for a hug and smelling of lilies, as usual. "Never you mind, Jessica." She gave Rayne and Ophelia a knowing look, her vivid, blue eyes conveying a silent message. "Your friends know the truth, and that's all that matters."

Not as reassuring as Nicolette, no doubt intended. Truth, Jessica had concluded during her short stint in London, seldom accounted for as much as titillating *on dit.*

Nicolette arced a long-fingered hand between herself and the other women. "Besides, our being here is part of a grand plan contrived by our ducal friends, their duchesses, and a few others who aren't to be trifled with. My mother, as well as my brother, also lend their support." She quirked her mouth into a wry smile. "Though as much as Ansley deigns society, that's not much help, I fear."

That was true. Ansley, Earl of Scarborough, was a unique man. Kind but subdued, and he tossed off nearly all social strictures in favor of his preferred interests and regimens.

Nicolette stepped aside so that Rayne could buss Jessica's cheek. More reserved than either Ophelia or Nicolette, she clasped Jessica's hands in her own. "Is it true? You're to wed Bainbridge?" A naughty grin tipped her mouth. "He is devilishly handsome."

How, precisely, had they learned that tidbit? Ah, part of the grand plan, no doubt.

"He's proposed, and I've accepted." No need for her to tell them neither of them had any choice in the matter. It was an unstated fact. No one with a lick of sense would attempt to spin a romantic slant on the situation.

Theadosia glided in and glanced around with satisfaction. "Excellent. I shall request tea. You girls are precisely what Jessica needs."

Her sister should chastise their friends for taking such a chance, but Jessica couldn't deny she was grateful they had. The fickle world of London Society seemed a trifle less daunting when surrounded by her dearest friends.

Subdued laughter and forced gaiety filled the next two hours. Everyone avoided mention of the puce hippopotamus in the room. Namely, the sordid events that had taken place at the ball. She could tell by their side-eyed glances they were dying to know the details but would bite off their tongues before asking.

Not ready to reveal all just yet—she mightn't ever be—Jessica studiously turned her attention away when she noticed their inquisitive gazes.

Finally, Nicolette peeked at the watch pinned to her spencer and released a loud, distinctly disgruntled sigh. "I'm loathe to be the one who puts an end to our lovely visit, but Mama wishes me to walk Belle in St James's Park with her this afternoon." She pulled a face. "Which means she's probably arranged for a gentleman or two or three to accidentally come upon us. Mayhap Belle will bark and growl and dispel any need for conversation."

The sweet-tempered pug was more likely to beg to be picked up and petted.

Nicolette still hadn't completely recovered from being jilted two years ago. She now viewed men as one would a pox sore or a carbuncle. Her mother, a consummate matchmaker, used ploy after ploy to introduce her most reluctant daughter to eligible gentleman.

And Nicolette, being Nicolette, rebuffed them all,

refusing to take a chance on love again.

Another round of hugs commenced, with many murmured assurances that all would be well, when in fact, each woman knew that wasn't precisely true. Jessica had only ever wanted to marry for love. Now her wedding gown was a shroud of ruination, her bridesmaid, a tarnished reputation. At least the groom was pleasing.

She looped her arm through the bend in Ophelia's elbow as they walked to the entrance.

Ophelia slowed her steps until they trailed several paces behind Rayne and Nicolette. Her soulful hazel eyes searched Jessica's. "Tell me true, dearest. How are you really? I cannot think you are happy to marry a stranger, no matter how handsome he might be."

"Miss Brighton is with child." Why had Jessica blurted that out?

Ophelia's eyes went round as the moon. "Oh no," she whispered, her voice equal parts aghast and stunned. She darted a swift glance at the other women then turned her head side to side, before hauling Jessica into a secluded corner. "What will you do? Is it…? Is it Bainbridge's?"

Jessica filled her lungs.

Is it?

No. She felt confident it wasn't. She released the breath in a whoosh and shook her head. "I'm confident it's not. I cannot explain how I know, but there's a decency in Crispin, which he conceals behind wastrel and libertine ramparts and bastions. He's not the sort who'd father a child on a woman and leave her to deal with the situation."

If he were such a cad, he wouldn't have offered for her. He'd have left her to deal with her tarnished reputation alone.

Jessica brushed her hair away from her face. "He kissed me."

Her blasted tongue seemed to have acquired a mind of its own today. The good Lord only knew what else might come spilling forth.

Ophelia's jaw went slack, practically hitting her bosom. Then a wide, delighted smile spread across her face. "And you *liked* it." Her grin widened, and she gave a little, excited hop. "You did! Why, Jessica

Miriam Emerald Brentwood, you liked it very much, indeed."

"I did." Oh, she had. Indeed, she had. She'd like to kiss Crispin again. And again. And again.

What would've happened if Victor hadn't interrupted? For certain, they'd not have ended up naked on the divan. Once in a lifetime was more than sufficient to be discovered as such.

Squinting, Ophelia glanced upward in concentration. "Forgive me for overstepping, but we *are* the dearest of friends, after all. I couldn't help but notice the way you've watched him these many months. And you admit you enjoyed his kiss. Aren't you a just little pleased about the match?"

More than a little pleased, and yet dismay also marred what should've been joyful anticipation.

"I am, but I wish the union weren't forced upon us." It didn't hurt to admit the truth to Ophelia. She'd guard the secret with her life. "It's not the ideal way to begin a marriage."

Jessica dropped her attention to her hands. Untold numbers of people before they had entered into arranged marriages and marriages of convenience and still had managed to carry on with their lives.

Yes, but many had also trudged along, wretched and bitterly unhappy.

"I'd hoped for a love match," she admitted, unable to keep the forlorn note from her voice.

"But..." Ophelia hesitated, her gaze keen and probing. "Oh. I see." She leaned near and drew Jessica into her arms. Offering the comfort only a dearest friend who knows one as well as one knows oneself can provide. The kind of friend who never judged but accepted and loved unconditionally. "You love him?"

Do I?

I do. I do. I truly do.

God, help me. That's what this...this turmoil is.

How could she not have been aware all these months?

This weighty, aching sensation wasn't at all how she'd anticipated love would feel. No rainbows and stars and gaiety. No dizzying sensations of floating. No sparkling eyes and incandescent smiles.

She'd expected a fluttering pulse whenever she'd

seen Crispin. For warmth to spiral outward from her middle when he spoke to her. His presence to muddle her thoughts and despondency to cloak her whenever they were apart.

What she felt at present was excruciatingly magnificent. An agony of splendor. A mélange of hurt and joy so entangled it was impossible to distinguish the pleasure from the pain.

She loved Crispin. Adored him.

When had it happened? How had it sneaked up on Jessica, catching her unawares?

How could she not have recognized falling in love with the seductive scoundrel?

Oh, love—*the tricky devil*—had wooed her. Won her.

Steadily. Stealthily. Slyly.

She was in the thrall of the insidious emotion. Snared, well and good. Much like a drunkard's dependence on spirits. The process wasn't instant or overnight. Nay. The twin demons of time and exposure gradually worked their wiles until, one day, one realized they craved the substance—were miserable without it.

Or as in her case, only felt whole when she was with Crispin.

Stupid. Stupid. Stupid. How could Jessica have been so foolish?

Blinking away the moisture stinging her eyes, Jessica gave a shaky, self-deprecating smile. “Is it that obvious?”

Likely, her dratted calf-eyed glances had given her away, despite her valiant efforts to mask her sentiments.

“No, it’s not, if that reassures you.” Ophelia stepped back, still holding Jessica’s forearms. Forehead furrowed, sympathy shone in her eyes. “You’re not happy about it, though, are you?”

Happy? Hardly. It was one thing to give her body to him.

But her heart? Her soul?

Such vulnerability terrified Jessica. She might very well lose herself, her identity, her self-respect.

“He doesn’t love me. Yes, he wants my body, but I’m not completely convinced a man such as he is capable of enduring fidelity, Ophelia, let alone love.”

12

A week after Brighton's unpleasant visit, Crispin marched up the six well-scrubbed steps to the Sutcliffes' ostentatious residence, complete with double doors painted a vibrant ruby-red. He was expected for tea, a guise to see Jessica contrived by him and the Duke and Duchess of Sutcliffe.

The stubborn woman had not called upon him again, which both relieved and exasperated him. Her absence provided an undistracted opportunity for his head to heal while he put mechanisms in place to prove Lilith Brighton and her father the bold-faced liars they were. It also gave him time to discover what foul hole Brookmoore had scuttled into or what rock he'd crawled beneath as well as report his crimes to the authorities.

Why, only this morning, his detectives had reported seeing Brookmoore slithering into his rented rooms, looking much the worse for wear.

Jessica, the maddening, darling woman, hadn't responded to his daily notes, and that worried him no small amount. He feared Brighton's libelous declaration had put her off. Raised qualms and questions.

Today, Crispin meant to set her straight on the matter.

He would've done so the day he proposed, but he'd all but passed out after Brighton's thunderous departure from the drawing room. Weak as a kitten, Sutcliffe supporting him on one side and Barlow on the other, he'd barely been able to raise his head to beg her pardon. To assure her, all would be well. That Brighton was lying through his yellow teeth.

Crispin had never even danced with Lilith Brighton, let alone bedded the chit. The notion repulsed him, making him realize all the more he could never have wed her and fathered a child on her. The dukedom would've gone to a distant cousin perched somewhere in the extensive family tree.

Pale, her delicate features taut, Jessica had stared at him, her gaze searching. Probing. Seeking. Not accusing, however. Several other emotions had flitted across her face: worry, fear, uncertainty, concern, doubt. The last lingered, shadowing her gorgeous blue-green eyes, and it was that uncertainty that lanced him afresh every time he summoned her exquisite face.

She didn't trust him. Why should she?

Because of their kiss. It had been unlike anything he'd ever experienced.

Even after their soul-shattering kiss, she had misgivings. It was only natural, he reminded himself. She couldn't know what they'd shared had been beyond rare, the fusing of spirits. Immediate. Unbreakable. Profound.

Why, he'd have scoffed at such tripe if he hadn't experienced it firsthand.

Jessica Brentwood was his. *His.* And, by damn, he was hers, whether she knew it or not.

He must somehow convince her she could trust him. That they could build a future together. The beginning might be a mite precarious, but that was no fault of theirs.

Brighton, the feckless bounder, had successfully planted a seed of suspicion. It stung how easily she'd believed the rotter, but Crispin couldn't blame her. She didn't know him well. He'd honed a devilish reputation, one he'd asked her to believe wasn't true without giving her any foundation for doing so.

Despite his doctor's orders that he should rest for a few more days, he'd left his house yesterday. There'd been a constant stream of people in and out he'd summoned since Brighton's harshly slung accusation, but there were tasks Crispin must attend to himself.

Only a niggling ache now annoyed him where the blow had fallen. That, and the blasted stitches. They itched something awful.

Since Jessica's departure, he'd been restless and edgy, needing to see her. Needing to assure himself she was well. Almost as if he anticipated Brighton or Brookmoore would spring another foul surprise upon him.

Or upon Jessica. Perchance both of them again.

He couldn't help but feel she wasn't entirely safe and had conveyed his concern to Sutcliffe. Rather than disregard Crispin's worries, Sutcliffe agreed to take additional security measures at home and when they ventured out.

Never before had Crispin felt such an overpowering need to protect another. To ensure someone's safety and wellbeing. There were no lengths to which he wouldn't go to safeguard Jessica. To make her his duchess.

Only, according to Sutcliffe, she hadn't peeked her delicate nose outdoors since she'd left Crispin's house the day he'd proposed. Evidently, upon their departure, they'd gone home by way of St. James's Park, after the duchess had insisted the fresh air might do her younger sister good.

Well acquainted with the workings of London Society, Sutcliffe had believed they ought to go directly home, but his wife was not to be dissuaded. The weather had been pleasant, and her grace had erroneously believed a turn about the park might lighten her sister's somber mood and lift her low spirits.

Jessica, in particular, was fond of the numerous fuzzy, dappled, ducklings paddling near Duck Island or drowsily sunning themselves upon the shore.

Crispin would have to see to it that he acquired a few ducklings and goslings for her to raise. A puppy, too, since that was what had lured her to the hothouse.

Until recently, the Duchess of Sutcliffe had also lived her entire life in a warm and welcoming community. Her inexperience with the sharp-tongued, critical *haut ton* had, most unfortunately, made her sister an easy target.

The outing, which was to have been followed by ices at Gunter's, had proved a colossal mistake, according to Sutcliffe. They'd encountered several members of the upper ten thousand, and Jessica had been given the cut direct by more than one.

Ladies had pulled their skirts aside while making blistering comments accompanied by smoldering looks of contempt. And, as Crispin had feared, many of the men had lewdly sized her up like a new type of pastry they couldn't wait to sample.

Sutcliffe cursed himself for a thousand kinds of fool for not anticipating what would happen. He'd honestly hoped that if Jessica were in his company, no one would dare turn a gimlet eye upon her.

He'd been dead wrong.

Which raised more concerns. *Le Beau Monde* had passed judgment, and it would take more than a duke's championing her to restore things to rights. The unpleasant encounter had only confirmed Crispin's suspicions.

There was no more time to delay. Arrangements must be made for their immediate marriage. It was astounding what quick nuptials could remedy. Crispin had seen that miracle work more than once, by God.

One day ruined and, the next, married and welcomed back into the *haut ton's* capricious bosom. Such bloody damn hypocrites. How many of those self-righteous pricks were sneaking in and out of bedchambers themselves? Most, truth be known. Or if they weren't now, they had in their heydays.

The banns were supposed to have been read two days after his proposal. But someone—probably that bastard Brighton—had whispered in the bishop's ear. Likely after *donating* a considerable sum to the Church.

More blasted hypocrisy.

Crispin squinted slightly and pulled his earlobe. Didn't Brighton have another connection to the Church? He couldn't precisely recall the exact nature, however. It would come to him eventually.

In any event, the man of God had refused to read the banns until the matter of the broken betrothal was resolved. The issue *was* resolved. Brighton's daughter had colluded with Brookmoore to ruin Jessica and smack Crispin over the head, and now the girl's belly swelled with Brookmoore's seed.

The contract was null. Void. Invalid. And Lilith had provided the means for the dissolution. As spelled out in elaborate detail on page seven, paragraph three.

The resignation in Jessica's eyes upon hearing Brighton's contemptible lie had nearly fractured his heart. Lilith Brighton was not the first woman to falsely accuse a man of fathering her child. In Crispin's case, he could prove he hadn't. When he explained the truth of it to Jessica, he was confident he'd reassure her. He must. He'd not wed her having her believe another woman carried his issue.

If he did, she'd see him as the basest sort of bastard.

Yesterday, he'd met with his man-of-affairs, his solicitor, and the investigators hired to poke around a bit about Brookmoore's clandestine meetings with Miss Brighton. It hadn't taken much sleuthing by the detectives to confirm the chit was indeed breeding.

Truthfully, it was somewhat astonishing, and not a little disturbing, what tattle might be learned from the mouths of domestics. Once located, Brightons' laundress confessed with alacrity—incentivized by a heavy coin purse—it had been months since she'd laundered any menstrual cloths in the Brighton household. At least since December, which meant Lilith Brighton was four months gone into her pregnancy and would show very soon.

The current fashions helped hide her swelling

belly, and that she was plump to start with also played to her advantage. No wonder she'd gone along with Brookmoore's scheme. Or had she concocted the plan and ensured the viscount's assistance with promises of a considerable dowry?

The blackguard's pockets were always to let, and he was in debt up to his inadequately starched neckcloth.

Was Brighton truly so stupid he couldn't add two and two—couldn't recall that Crispin had wintered at his country estate? His servants could attest to that. He'd also attended Sutcliffe's Christmastide house party and dozens more country assemblies over the past few months, including Twistleton's musical soiree in March.

He could produce dozens of witnesses to swear he'd not left the country or been seen in London. Unlike the majority of the upper ten thousand, the Brightons lived in London year-round. Brighton ought to have considered those details before slinging false accusations at him.

Unless the man knew and didn't bloody well care.

That seemed more the gist of it. Why settle for a viscount, even if he had compromised Lilith?

Crispin had refused to be bullied into marrying the girl before, but now that she'd spread her legs for Brookmoore… He snorted, loudly and contemptuously. Satan would be making snow angels in hell before Lilith Brighton became his duchess.

He damn well wasn't marrying her and essentially proclaiming to all and sundry the child she carried was his. For God's sake, she might well bear a male child; no by-blow of Brookmoore's would inherit the Bainbridge dukedom.

It certainly did make one wonder if both Brookmoore and Lilith had taken leave of their senses. Their plot was doomed to failure from the beginning. They would've had to have killed him to prevent him from naming them as the guilty parties.

His wound took that moment to twinge. Mayhap killing him had been their intent. Had they succeeded, Jessica would've been left with no defense whatsoever.

A grimace twisted his mouth. Why hadn't he considered that before? Because no man liked to think his betrothed detested him so much, she'd conspire to see him dead.

Brighton wouldn't spread word of his daughter's delicate condition. Not if he wanted to maintain his position on Society's outer fringes. He'd not been so foolish as to have Lilith examined by a physician or midwife either. Crispin's detectives had explored those avenues thoroughly.

Nonetheless, except for bribing the bishop, Brighton had been eerily silent. It raised Crispin's hackles. He had no doubt the blighter was plotting. But what?

As he rapped upon the bright door, he looked up and down the street. Several people regarded him with avid curiosity. A few haughty matrons lifted their chins and turned their faces away, but the men smiled or winked. The double-standard galled. Women snubbed Jessica, and men admired Crispin's prowess, and yet they were each as much a victim as the other.

He meant to coax her out of her self-imposed isolation. A trip to Gunter's was in order for a long-overdue ice. The more they were seen together, the more credibility would be given to his break with Miss Brighton and his betrothal to Jessica.

Crispin had no druthers about revealing Lilith's little secret. In fact, he was prepared to make her condition very public if Brighton didn't cooperate. He'd wait until his investigators had gathered all of the relevant facts to make his case impenetrable. Blackmailing a peer wouldn't weigh in her or her father's favor.

Dandridge, Pennington, Westfall, Asherford, Sheffield, Waycross, and several other friends and members of *Bon Chance* had vowed their support. No one was fool enough to take on a dozen powerful dukes.

He rapped again, surprised the door hadn't opened at once.

Did Jessica ride?

He flicked a speck of dust off his lapel. He'd never observed her riding in Colechester, but then again, her family was as poor as proverbial church mice. He rather imagined she'd enjoy his stables at Pickford Hill Park. There was something satisfying when a foal was born. As if Crispin had contributed something pure and innocent and useful to this wretched world.

The door finally opened, and Sutcliffe's bland-faced butler ushered him inside. Ah, he'd forgotten Rumsfeld never rushed at anything. Steady as she goes and slow as a tortoise. Or a snail. Through molasses. In wintertime.

"Good day, Rumsfeld."

"Your Grace," Rumsfeld, intoned in his usual monotone. After accepting his hat, gloves, and cane, the butler laid them aside and closed the door. Each movement slow and methodical. He lifted a gloved hand, the gesture practiced and perfected to convey haughty deference. "This way, if you please," he droned, sounding rather like an oversized, lazy bumblebee.

Crispin quirked a cynical eyebrow. His butler was stodgy and stuffy, but Rumsfeld made him seem like a drunken court jester.

"I do know the way, Rumsfeld." He couldn't resist teasing.

"Indeed." Rumsfeld returned without breaking his measured stride or inflecting any emotion into his voice. Momentarily, they arrived at the salon. "His Grace, the Duke of Bainbridge," he proclaimed, in the same tones one would deliver a deadly diagnosis.

Before he finished announcing his arrival, Crispin sought Jessica. She sat beside her sister, her flaxen hair twisted into a loose chignon at the back of her head. A few brazen curls had escaped their confines and lay teasingly over her shell-like ears.

Today, she wore pink and white—fresh as a morning rosebud—and a matching ribbon graced the crown of her head and was tied at her shapely nape. Dark bluish-purple smudges shadowed her eyes, which, to his immense satisfaction, lit at the sight of him.

She'd never looked lovelier, and he wished he had the right to take her into his arms and kiss her until the worry left her precious features. Until she was relaxed and went all feminine softness against him. Until she believed there'd never be another woman for him.

Poised, a practiced, benign smile arching her

kissable mouth, she met his regard. Hope and something undefinably warm shone in her aquamarine eyes.

Crispin's pulse kicked up a notch in anticipation. Perhaps he hadn't given her enough credit, and she hadn't believed Brighton's drivel after all.

He returned her smile, putting into it all he couldn't say aloud. Not here and now. Later, if he was permitted a few minutes alone with her.

James Brentwood stood at his entrance and bowed. "Bainbridge."

"Brentwood." What the devil was Jessica's brother doing here?

Brentwood resumed his seat, appearing anything but relaxed. Unusual for him. Even though he'd chosen law as his profession and possessed a brilliant mind, he tended to be good-natured, though never jovial.

Neither was he a rogue, who with his looks and flush pockets, he might've been. There'd been a woman, years ago, if Crispin recalled correctly. She'd jilted him for a duke.

He possessed the same blue-green eyes as Jessica,

but whereas his sisters had light hair, his was a rich auburn.

Recently, Brentwood had dabbled in several lucrative, very successful investments. He had an uncanny nose for sniffing out unusual, profitable ventures, and Sutcliffe and Crispin had both engaged in fruitful business dealings with him.

Today, pensive and somber, he appeared ready to present a criminal defense case in court.

"Come, Your Grace." The duchess waved him toward an empty chair. "Have a seat. I believe you prefer your tea plain?"

"Yes, please, and do address me as Crispin or, if you must, Bainbridge. We are to be family, after all."

The smile affixed to her face never faltered, but he didn't miss the strained look that passed between Brentwood and Sutcliffe.

Jessica busied herself with stirring her tea—she took hers with milk and sugar—and then she set the spoon aside and took a sip before meeting his eyes again. "Your Grace—"

"Crispin," he corrected, refusing to fall back into

starchy formality. The room fairly crackled with unspoken tension. He accepted his cup of tea and, as he raised it to his mouth, asked, "Why is everyone so Friday-faced?"

Scratching his nape, Sutcliffe grimaced. "We've run into a bit of a snag."

"I'm aware Brighton bribed the clergy at my parish, if that's what you refer to." Crispin relaxed into the chair, hooking one knee over the other. "I should've expected it. I always like to believe men of God are above such machinations, but they're only human, and at times temptation—"

At the crushed expression washing over Jessica's face, he could've bitten his tongue. *Blast and damn.*

The duchess saved him from his blunder. "It is disappointing." She referred to her father, he'd wager. "I suppose, just like everyone else, they justify their sins."

"As you know, I petitioned for a special license on your behalf, as you requested." Brentwood leaned forward and accepted tea from his sister, neatly changing the subject. "It was denied. I suspected when the archbishop took so long to approve the request, that would be the case."

"It seems Brighton's reach is farther than I anticipated." Irritation, sharp and swift washed over Crispin.

"His brother is a close confidant of the archbishop," Sutcliffe offered, crossing his legs.

Ah, there was that connection Crispin hadn't been able to identify earlier.

"So no special license and no reading of the banns in London." He angled toward Jessica. "I suppose that means we'll have to journey to Colechester and wed in your old parish by common license. I regret the inconvenience, but it cannot be helped."

He'd plant Brighton a facer if he were present, older man or not. How dare he manipulate him? He'd learn soon enough he'd taken on the wrong foe.

Would it be difficult for Jessica to marry in Colechester? The parish had been her father's before he was disgraced. Or would she welcome the opportunity? To be wed in familiar surroundings?

Her chest rose and fell with a long sigh. "James just came from there. The new vicar won't perform the ceremony, either. I had hoped to escape London—"

Bloody damn hell.

That left Scotland. And they all knew it.

Holding her gaze, he said, "It's to be Scotland, then."

13

Jessica forced what she hoped was a tranquil mien to her face and took another long sip of tea. Her life had tumbled teakettle over spout in a week. After her treatment in St. James's Park, she never wanted to set foot anywhere in London again. Never wanted to encounter the critical, mean-spirited denizens of High Society who'd taken it upon themselves to judge her.

In fact, the urge to pack her trunks and flee to Ridgewood Court, Victor's country estate, and never show her face in public again sounded quite lovely indeed. Then, that part of her which rebelled at unjustness reared up and refused to let her take such a cowardly route.

Jessica hadn't done anything wrong. She was the victim, dash it all.

Nonetheless, Hammon Brighton was a greater, more cunning adversary than Crispin or Victor had anticipated. With relative ease, he'd made it impossible for her and Crispin to wed in England. The man wasn't a peer of the realm, yet his powerful hand was far-reaching. Wealth and bribery trumped position and status in this case, it seemed.

Firming her mouth against the disgust riddling her, she stared into her teacup.

She didn't believe Crispin had fathered Miss Brighton's child. The girl had proven herself to be a liar and manipulator. Foolish and rash, she'd been seduced, no doubt. And then, when her lover had abandoned her, she wrongly believed she could falsely accuse Crispin to save her skin. She was beneath contempt.

Or perhaps Lilith Brighton wasn't behind the false claim. Mayhap her sire was.

A thought struck with the sharpness of a well-honed arrow. Perhaps she wasn't with child at all.

How awful to be the progeny of a man who'd force her to wed someone she didn't want to. Daughters were little more than pawns and possessions, and God help the women whose fathers used them as such.

Jessica cut a covert glance to Theadosia. She'd faced a similar unpleasant fate, and their father had been—*was*—a vicar. He should've been above such maneuverings. Thank God above, Victor had rescued her sister.

Who, pray tell, would rescue Jessica?

Did she want rescuing?

Through half-lowered lashes, she peeked at Crispin. He seemed surprisingly at ease. Confident and self-assured. And a softness, a gentleness, tempered his features.

It wasn't that Jessica objected to a match with him. She didn't. She'd have preferred a courtship, and a bit of wooing by the wicked duke—who wasn't so very wicked after all—wouldn't have gone amiss. Nonetheless, one persistent, aggravating thought continued to plague her; would he ever have considered her for his duchess if this situation hadn't forced them together?

Jessica wanted to believe Crispin would have done. He'd claimed a long-held attraction to her. But the truth of it was dukes didn't marry country nobodies or vicars' daughters. At least he'd receive her substantial dowry, thanks to Victor's generosity.

Dear Victor. He'd treated her as a beloved younger sister.

"I'd hoped elopement to Scotland wouldn't be necessary," Theadosia said quietly, a pinched look about her eyes as she sliced a distressed glance to Victor.

Jessica's heart twinged. So had she. She wouldn't pretend eloping to Gretna Green didn't distress her. It did, but what alternative was there? She could at least voice her objection.

"And what if *I* don't wish to elope to Scotland?" There she'd said it. "It makes me so angry those *people* are forcing our hand."

"We've exhausted the other possibilities, Jessica," Crispin said, not unkindly. His perceptive gaze narrowed the merest bit, shrewdness replacing his earlier ease. "Unless you've changed your mind."

Theadosia cut him an appalled look. "She cannot."

"And I did not," Jessica said with more heat than she'd intended. "I simply resent having no control in any of this." She waved her hand in a circle in the air. "You're making all of these plans, and not once have any of you consulted me. This is my life."

"At this juncture," her sister said cautiously, "Scotland appears the only viable option, Jessica. Naturally, we shall accompany you."

As if that made everything well and good.

Victor gave a sharp nod, although his stern expression didn't relax.

Did he worry the journey was too much for Theadosia's delicate condition? The babe wasn't due for another three months, and they needn't dash pell-mell to Scotland. A more sedate pace might be set, which would accommodate her health, yet the concern couldn't be overlooked or dismissed.

How could she contemplate all of this with such cool detachment? *How?* Because if she permitted the whorl of emotions and feelings bubbling ever higher behind her ribs to escape, she'd become a distraught, watering pot. And blubbering and weeping would serve no purpose—

would change nothing and only serve to make her appear weak.

"How soon should we depart?" Theadosia asked. "Should I order the staff to prepare our trunks? Or do we need to travel light? Perhaps just a valise with the barest essentials?"

James set his teacup down then ran a finger down the side of his nose. His features settled into his solicitor's expression.

Ah, he was about to present an argument.

"I'd recommend two coaches be prepared," he said. "Bainbridge's, containing decoys—Theadosia and Sutcliffe—which will set out first but ramble around the outskirts of London for a few hours. And another unmarked conveyance with myself, Bainbridge, and Jessica. We shall be accompanied by armed outriders that will join us once on the road north."

That pronouncement set Jessica back on her heels. Was there truly such a need for deception? Or armed outriders? She hadn't considered that.

She didn't like this turn of events in the least. "What if Brighton arranges to have their coach waylaid? I shan't have Theadosia or the baby discommoded or endangered."

"I agree with Brentwood. Two coaches are wise." Crispin leaned forward, catching Jessica's attention. Encouragement and kindness glinted in those pearl-gray eyes. A gleam of emotion decidedly more combustible glittered in those tantalizing depths, too. "If your sister's coach is stopped—and I suspect Brighton might be imprudent enough to attempt such an ill-conceived act—the men we'll hire to protect your sister and Sutcliffe will close in on them."

He looked at James and Victor for confirmation. They both nodded their assent.

"I'll be armed as well," Victor said, his features gone fierce.

Her sister looked rather ill, and Jessica couldn't blame her.

"This sounds much too dangerous to me," she objected. She'd never have believed it could be so challenging to wed. The danger, plotting, and subterfuge stripped their elopement of any hint of romance. "How do you intend to protect Theadosia and Victor if Brighton or his henchmen become aggressive?"

"They'll be detained," Crispin said, as if it were the simplest, most logical of things. "And Sutcliffe will decide what should be done with them for accosting a duke and his duchess. It won't go well for them if they are foolish enough to act so recklessly."

"And I," James announced, giving Crispin a hard stare before turning a tender gaze upon her, "shall act as chaperone and assure no one can contest the legitimacy of your vows. No blacksmith's anvil for these two." He levered two fingers between her and Crispin. "They'll have a proper church ceremony conducted by a man of God."

Theadosia's face fell. "But I wanted to be present at Jessica's wedding." She tossed her husband a helpless look. "Especially since our parents aren't here."

Jessica couldn't prevent the resentment billowing inside her toward the Brightons and Brookmoore. Their selfish actions had wreaked havoc on more lives than just hers and Crispin's. Not only was she being denied a proper wedding with her friends in attendance, her beloved sister wouldn't even be there to witness the ceremony.

Tears threatened, but she doggedly willed them to subside. None of them were choosing this path. Circumstances and evil people had forced this course upon them.

Don't forget it's a forced wedding, too.

Not precisely forced, but most certainly one of inconvenience.

James shook his head. "You'll need to pretend to be Jessica, Thea. You look enough alike that you can pull it off. I've thought about this the entire journey back from Colechester. Brighton has gone to great extremes to prevent our sister and Bainbridge from wedding. And we all know how essential it is that the ceremony takes place as soon as possible. Granted, his claim that his daughter is breeding complicates the matter, but that's Brighton's problem."

That was true enough. Did Brighton honestly think Crispin would marry his daughter now? The man was dicked in the nob if he did.

"He's mad enough to try something devious," Victor murmured as he settled on the settee beside his wife and took her hand, offering her comfort.

"The fruit didn't fall far from the tree in that family, did it?" Jessica quipped, amazed she could do so. "One bad apple and all that rot."

Four pairs of eyes swung to her, but it was Crispin's that held her gaze. A glint of humor sparked there. He'd understood the poor pun and her failed attempt at humor to lighten the mood.

Warmth burgeoned within her. He understood her as no one else ever had. It strengthened the connection she felt with him. Made her want to be alone with him to explore it further.

"Brentwood is right," he said, giving a considering nod. "I wouldn't put anything past Brighton."

Could this become any more ridiculous? Or

scandalous? Or infuriating?

Jessica cleared her throat, heartily regretting ever coming to London. She'd take the country's sedate pace and lack of intrigue any day. Give her chickens, a library, paints and a canvas, and a puppy, and she'd be content.

Poppydash and codscock.

"So, where does that leave us?" she asked.

"We must depart for Scotland as soon as possible. The extra men to protect the coaches can be arranged for today, and I'll alert the authorities to our suspicions." Crispin took her hand, giving the fingers a gentle squeeze. "I know marrying in Scotland isn't what you wanted."

Tenderness and understanding softened the corners of his eyes.

"It's not what you wanted, either." How awkward to have this discussion in front of others.

"Perhaps we should permit Bainbridge and Jessica a few moments of privacy?" Theadosia suggested, ever the considerate hostess and always able to discern Jessica's innermost thoughts.

Victor looked as though he was about to object, but after leveling Crispin a stern glance conceded. "Very well. We'll adjourn to my study to work out the details. Join us there when you are finished."

"I'll instruct our maids to pack." Theadosia arched a winged eyebrow. "I presume at some point *someone* will inform me when we are to depart?" she murmured dryly.

"Yes, my pet," Victor assured her, wrapping an arm about her thick waist.

James rose then, in an uncharacteristic public display of affection, bent and kissed the crown of Jessica's head. "All will be well, little sister."

Easy for him to say. It wasn't his life in turmoil.

With a wink and a fond smile, he followed their sister and brother-in-law from the room, leaving the door cracked behind him for propriety.

The room remained silent for several minutes after their departure.

"Are you having second thoughts, Jessica?" Crispin didn't accuse but seemed genuinely concerned.

Third and fourth thoughts, too. But it made no

difference. How could it possibly feel worse to marry Crispin now that she knew she loved him? Shouldn't it make the decision easier?

If he felt the same for her, it would've done.

"No." Jessica met his gaze with courage and strength. As she'd determined earlier, he'd not find her a weak, feckless female. "And I do not believe you are the father of Miss Brighton's child." Straightforward and to the point. Instinct told her Crispin needed to know that truth.

"I am not," he said, vehemence ringing in his voice. "And, if necessary, I can prove I remained in residence at my estate except for your sister's Christmastide house party."

She'd hoped for as much. Had, in fact, had similar thoughts, but to hear him proclaim his proof of innocence brought a flood of relief. Mr. Brighton could blather his lies about town, but Crispin had evidence to the contrary.

"Crispin, might I ask you something personal?" She brushed a finger over her eyebrow, behind which a minor ache had begun to make itself known. Adjusting the pillow at her back, she relaxed against the settee. If she were here, Mama would frown at her poor posture.

Heavens. Poor posture was nothing considering what had transpired these past few days.

Surprise lifted his eyebrows, but he nodded, his expression grave. "Of course. I'd have honesty between us, always. I believe honesty and trust are more important than love for a healthy marriage. Love and passion ebb and flow, but a union built on a solid foundation of trust will never crumble."

When had he become so philosophical? And why did his words make her ridiculously emotional? A lump the size of the African continent formed in her throat, and moisture blurred her eyes for a second.

I shall not cry.

"What is it you wish to know?" Expectancy and kindness warmed his slate-gray eyes.

In for a penny, in for a pound. Jessica bolstered her courage.

"You claimed that if you'd not been betrothed to Miss Brighton, you'd have asked to pay your addresses to me. Forgive me, but I cannot help but believe you were being gallant, trying to alleviate the awkwardness of the moment." Noble and chivalrous. Putting her needs before his own. Attempting to make her feel somewhat less than an unwelcome, unworthy, and an unwanted burden. "What else were you to say, after all?"

"I'm furious. I shall resent you for all of the days of our lives. Marriage to you is not of my choosing, but my damnable honor requires me to offer for you?"

"You are a kind man. A generous man," she went on. *Two more reasons why I love you beyond everything.* "I've known that for several months." But she'd also known him to be a rake, so she'd disregarded his more exceptional qualities.

Wasn't that just like people—to focus on someone's faults rather than the myriad of other noteworthy qualities they might have?

His steady gaze never wavered from her, nor did he attempt to interrupt. Another thing she appreciated about him. He listened to her. Really listened.

"You said what needed to be said at that moment to protect my feelings. I'm grateful." Jessica offered a half-smile as she ran her fingers along the carved edge of the settee. "I truly am. But you must know by now, I'm no wilting flower. I shan't dissolve into tears or become faint from hearing the truth."

Blast. Babbling again.

"Jessica?" Did a note of humor resonate in his tone? Impatience mayhap? "What, precisely, are you trying to say?"

No more dillydallying or beating around the bush. Frankness and candidness. Yes, well, that was far easier to contemplate than actually to do. "I realize it's none of my—ah—*business,*" she said, struggling for the right words. "Except for that, we are betrothed—in a fashion."

"In a *fashion*?" Mockery toggled his hawkish eyebrows together, creating a deep groove above his nose.

She chose to ignore his sarcasm and went on as if he hadn't interjected. With a little wave of her hand, she said, "But if you hadn't been betrothed to Miss Brighton since you were a child, and if these difficult circumstances hadn't arisen, compelling you to offer for me, is there a woman you would've chosen to be your duchess of your own free will?"

His ducal duty required him to wed and sire an heir. Perchance he'd have waited a few more years to traipse down matrimony's convoluted path, after the dissolution of his betrothal with Miss Brighton, but he'd have done so eventually. Crispin wasn't the caliber of man to forsake his duty to the Bainbridge dukedom.

Perhaps a woman *had* captured his heart.

A powerful wave of unanticipated envy stabbed her.

His lady love would be exquisite, of course. Sweet tempered—the epitome of grace and refinement. And beautiful. How could she not be?

She'd sing like a songbird. Jessica did not have a voice, to her mother's chagrin.

No doubt Crispin's lady rode magnificently, too. Jessica had never sat a horse.

Cataloging his sweetheart's attributes while simultaneously listing her inadequacies made her rather ill. The tea threatened to curdle in her stomach, and despair lanced her heart.

If Crispin married her out of obligation, he'd never be able to make his true love his own, now that he was finally free of his commitment to Lilith Brighton. Life was most unfair. Or fate or providence or the divine powers. Whoever, or whatever, was responsible for this bumblebroth had no sense of justice.

But now he had an opportunity for true happiness.

She must forsake her own to allow him that chance. *I must, even if it shatters my heart.* Having never loved anyone except him, she couldn't imagine how distressing it would be to adore him as she did, and yet circumstances required her to wed another.

How awful. Frustrating and infuriating. *Heartbreaking.* God, how she wanted to curl into a ball of misery and wail her anguish. How could her heart keep beating? Her lungs continue to draw air?

He gazed at her for so long, his sultry gray eyes charcoal-dark and those sinfully thick eyelashes partially lowered, she feared she'd overstepped.

Jessica, you dim-witted dolt. Of course she'd

overstepped. Waded in, chest high. Chin high. She might very well drown in her foolhardiness. On her attempt at thoughtfulness and consideration. Because, above all else, she wanted Crispin to be happy.

It shouldn't hurt so bloody awful to love someone.

And still, he remained unnervingly silent, his expression intense and reflective. The seconds expanded, and with every punctuating *tick-tock* of the clock, she increasingly wished she could retract the intrusive question.

She didn't want to know.

Yes, I do.

No, it would hurt far too much.

I must know. Hers and Crispin's futures depended upon it.

His subtle cologne wreaked havoc on her senses, and his enticing heat drew her to him. Even now, she felt herself leaning toward him, attracted as if he were a magnet. Why must he be so mysterious and sexy? She could scarcely cobble two thoughts together when he was this close.

At last, he spoke, guardedly, as if considering his

words with great care. "There *is* someone. Has been for some time."

Jessica pointed her gaze to the floor for a second, lest he see the devastation in her eyes. Her blasted, so-easy-to-read eyes.

"A remarkable, intelligent, beautiful woman," he went on. "I would've made her mine in a heartbeat, had I been free to do so." His voice dropped to that husky tone that curled her toes and made her want to crawl atop him, nuzzle her nose in his corded neck, and run her fingers over the light stubble darkening his rugged jaw.

Such excruciating pain lanced her heart; he might've pierced her with a rusty, double-edged sword. Somehow, she husbanded her composure and kept from doubling over and clutching her chest. Jessica forced her focus upward to meet his gaze. She'd asked and had insisted upon honesty. Far better to have the truth out in the open.

"Does she know of your regard? Does she return it?" My, how composed she sounded, considering her impaled heart oozed blood. In truth, she was acting a rude snoop.

"I've never told her." The corners of his beautiful eyes softened, and a small smile arched his mouth. That splendid mouth that had plundered hers mere days ago. "I hope she feels the same about me, but she's never said so. There's not been an opportunity for us to declare ourselves."

The only thing standing between Crispin and this woman he loved was her. Well, the Brightons were a hindrance, but he had them well in hand. He had waited long enough to be happy.

"It saddens me that you have been stripped of a choice of spouse again, Crispin." She clenched her fingers and somehow marshaled the fortitude for what she needed to say, fully aware of the consequences. She would lose everything.

Everything.

Yes, but it would be worth it, for *he* would gain everything.

"I release you from your proposal. I'd rather you found joy with her."

14

Crispin's heart nearly exploded with love and admiration, and he struggled to check a burst of exuberant laughter.

"My foolish, adorable darling." He swept her onto his lap, grinning at her startled squeak of surprise. He kissed her forehead. "Darling, adorable fool." Pressing his lips to her left cheek, he murmured, "Sweetheart." And then he whisked his mouth over her neglected right cheek. "*You,* my sweet Jessica, are that woman."

Clutching his arms, she blinked up at him, her wonder-filled eyes the color of the sea after the sun had disappeared from the horizon. "I am?" Her words came out in a hushed whisper. "Truly?"

"Truly, my love." He brushed his mouth across her incredibly soft lips. "My only love. Ever."

Did she understand what he was saying?

That he loved her?

Had for so very long.

And now, at last, Crispin was free to tell her. To tell her everything he'd secreted in his heart, and, *by God*, as soon as the vows were exchanged, he'd show her with his mouth and hands and body.

He'd worship every velvety inch of her, and when he finished, she'd have no more doubts that she, alone, was the woman of his heart. Had always been and would always be.

"I wasn't simply being kind when I told you that I'd have courted you had I been free, Jessica." He traced a finger down her satin-soft cheek. "From the first time I saw you, I knew you were special. But I could only admire you from afar. Wishing, always hoping but never expecting, that you might actually be mine someday."

Nestling closer, Jessica wrapped one arm around his waist. She looped the other behind his neck and rested her cheek against his chest. "I noticed you, too. But as I said before, your reputation put me off. I didn't want to be another silly, infatuated girl who'd succumbed to your charms."

"My charms, eh?" He waggled his eyebrows as he crooked his finger and nudged her chin upward.

She gave his hair a slight tug, which also caused her generous bum to press into his loins. God help him. "You know full well, Crispin Harlow Benjamin Rolston, Duke of Bainbridge, what powerful affect you have on women."

"Do I?" he replied in his most seductive voice. "Why don't you show me?"

Their lips nearly touched, and as he spoke, he lowered his head, until but a hair's breadth remained between them. Her vanilla-and-clove scent wafted around Crispin, warm and inviting. Sensual and sultry. Sweet and spicy, just like the incredible woman in his arms.

With a little sigh, Jessica angled her chin upward until their mouths met. This wasn't the scorching, passionate kiss of a couple of days ago. This was two souls coming together, revealing what they'd hidden from the world and each other for so long.

He loved her. Loved this golden-haired, marine-eyed marvel of a woman. He spanned his hands across her narrow waist, worshipping her as he'd yearned to do for so long.

Soft and sweet and perfect, her mouth moved beneath his.

His adoration tempered his passion as he tenderly, reverently explored the sweet hollows, allowing his hand to roam the contours and curves of her lush form. There wasn't anything he wouldn't do to keep her safe. To make her his.

Crispin lifted his head, taking in her heavy-lidded gaze and kiss-swollen, slightly red and damp lips. He stifled a groan and the urge to plunder her mouth once more. There'd be time for that later. After they left London behind.

The trip to Scotland might bloody well kill him.

Mayhap Brentwood could be persuaded to ride atop with the driver or, better yet, upon a mount. There was about as much chance of that happening as

Brighton coming to his senses.

Eyes glistening with emotion, she pressed her palm to his jaw.

"I love you, Jessica," he said simply. "I love you. I love you. *I love you.*"

There wasn't any need to embellish the declaration with poetic phrases or nonsensical fluff. He loved her. *I love you, Jessica.* Those four words were more potent than anything else he could say. She'd made a home for herself in his mind, his heart, and his soul.

Her gold-tipped lashes trembled as a joyful smile wreathed her face. "I love you, too."

A hint of the shy young woman he'd first met all those months ago in Colechester peered back at him, but an intrepid woman's gaze held his. A strong, intelligent woman. A woman who knew her mind and who would make him the ideal partner.

He kissed her nose, running his hands down the fine pink silk covering her spine. "I suppose we ought to join the others and finalize the arrangements. I'd like to depart for Scotland before dawn tomorrow."

She gave a small, regretful nod. "I wish we could marry here with our friends and family in attendance, but I understand why we cannot." A frown marred her smooth forehead. "Do you think Mr. Brighton will continue to give us trouble afterward?"

"He may try, but there'd be no point." Crispin helped her off his lap then stood, a distinct bulge pressing at the falls of his pantaloons. "I've had my solicitor send him a firmly worded note explaining point-by-point what crimes his daughter committed. They are serious, and it could be argued that she was an accessory to attempted murder."

Jessica gasped and paled, one hand flying to press against the hollow of her throat. "Do you think Brookmoore intended to kill you?"

He lifted a shoulder. "I cannot say. But I am prepared to bring charges against him, and the evidence supports such a claim. Brighton will not want his daughter to go to prison or risk deportation or hanging." He pulled his waistcoat and jacket into place. "If he's wise, he'll remove her to the country or marry her off to some ancient decrepitude who won't mind she's breeding."

Crispin extended his hand, and Jessica placed hers in it. Helping her rise, he didn't release the fine-boned fingers. He brushed his thumb over her ring finger. "I have something for you, Kitten." He fished around in his coat pocket and withdrew a sapphire velvet box. After lifting the lid, he held it out for her to inspect the contents.

A soft sigh parted her lips. "Oh, Crispin."

Two white diamonds sandwiched a square-cut, bluish-green-hued emerald.

"Will you put it on, please?" She extended her hand.

Once he'd lifted the ring from its white satin nest, he slipped the band on her finger. He held her fingers firmly in his. "Jessica, darling, will you marry me? Because I love you, and you love me? And nothing else matters?" Unfamiliar moisture blurred his vision. How he loved her. "Whatever the future brings, we'll face it together," he said huskily.

Her lower lip trembled as if she struggled to contain her emotions, as well. "I shall, Crispin. Gladly and unreservedly."

The tread of swift footsteps reverberating in the hallway caused him to retreat a step, to put a respectable distance between them. Sutcliffe and his duchess swept into the drawing room, strain evident on their faces.

"Where's James?" Jessica looked past her sister to the empty doorway.

"A messenger came 'round. James had to leave at once, but he vowed he'd be back as soon as possible," the duchess said, appearing rather wan.

"There's a message for you as well, Bainbridge." Sutcliffe veered Jessica a guarded look. "From one of your investigators." He raised the sealed paper.

Until that moment, Crispin hadn't noticed the rectangle.

The duchess held out her hands as she crossed to her sister. "Come, my dear. Have a seat and permit the duke to read his message."

Jessica placed her hands in her sister's and allowed her to guide her to a bench before a bay window. The sky had cleared, and only a few slightly ash-tinged clouds marred the azure horizon. She shook her head when the duchess urged her to claim a seat. "I'd prefer to stand, please. But Thea, you should sit. You appear as if you might faint."

The duchess gave a weak laugh. "I *am* a little shaken," she said as she folded onto the tufted crimson cushion. "But I do not faint any more than you do."

There was always a first time. In her delicate condition, the duchess shouldn't be exposed to all of these disconcerting happenings. Except, if she were anything like her strong-willed sister, she'd not be toddled off to rest, content to let others handle any unpleasantness.

A slight grin tipped Crispin's mouth. Thank God for strong-minded women.

"I take it, you know the contents of Crispin's missive?" Jessica's dubious gaze examined the note.

"I have a fair notion." The glitter of Jessica's ring caught her eye, and she grasped her sister's hand. "Oh my. It's simply lovely, dear. Emeralds have always been your favorite. And the color is so unique." She held Jessica's hand up to the window's light. "The stone has a slight bluish tint."

"It does, and I adore the square cut." A soft smile played around Jessica's mouth. A pretty, sweet, pink mouth which he very much wanted to kiss again.

The duchess slid him an assessing look.

Turning the letter over, Crispin broke the seal with his thumb. "I take it whatever is in here is what has caused you to look so glum?"

With a cautious glance toward the women, Sutcliffe gave a stiff nod. "It's either excellent or terrible news, depending on your perspective."

"As serious as all that?" It must be. Sutcliffe was a virtually, unflappable pillar. The tight lines bracketing his mouth and the taut look about his eyes suggested the letter's contents were of great import and impact. Brow lifted questioningly, Crispin unfolded the sheet. Angling his back toward the women, he perused the contents. His gut knotted, and a low oath escaped him between tight lips. "Good God!"

He shot an astounded glance over his shoulder as he refolded the letter then tucked it inside his pocket.

Sutcliffe responded with another tight nod. "Thea

knows. James's correspondence was similar. He went to assure no one altered the crime scene before the authorities arrived."

That explained the duchess's chalk-white face when she'd entered.

"Do you wish to tell Jessica, or would you prefer her sister or myself do so?" Sutcliffe asked beneath his breath.

"All that intense whispering is only making me more anxious," Jessica said starchily. "Since the three of you are aware, might not I also be apprised of whatever it is that has everyone looking so morose?"

Crispin didn't miss the hint of trepidation in her tone. He crossed to her and, after taking her hands in his, urged her to sit beside her sister. "We've just had word that Brookmoore was found murdered. Shot in the heart."

She blanched, her confused gaze racing from person to person. "Brighton?"

He shook his head. "No. Lilith killed him. She's…" He glanced to the duchess.

"She's taken leave of her senses, poor girl." Her

grace patted her sister's knee. "It was all too much for her. When he discarded her, and her father still insisted she wed Bainbridge, she must've decided to seek Brookmoore out. Who knows what transpired between them, but the fact that she went with a loaded pistol suggests her intent."

Brookmoore deserved to be shot after seducing, impregnating, and abandoning the girl.

"What will happen to her?" Though Jessica had every right to be furious with Lilith, only compassion colored her words. She bit her lower lip. "Her poor parents. Especially her mother."

Crispin could sympathize with Mrs. Brighton. Her overbearing husband had bullied her for as long as he could recall. To have her only child commit another crime, this one a hanging offense, the woman would be beside herself.

He, however, wasn't as benevolent as Jessica. Brighton was partially responsible for his daughter's plight. The controlling bugger had manipulated and coerced Lilith her entire life. Perhaps she'd thought she loved Brookmoore, and when he tossed her aside like an old shoe, her mind had snapped.

"I expect she'll be committed." Sutcliffe offered. "Brighton's pockets are deep enough, and he'll likely be able to arrange for a private facility."

"What of the baby?" Jessica asked.

"It's difficult to say." Her sister looked pensive. "If she carries it to term—and she may not—then I suppose her parents will determine whether they take the child in, foster it out, or put it in an orphanage."

"Even though her part in what she did to Crispin and me was unforgivable," Jessica shook her head, her earrings swaying with the motion, "I cannot help but feel pity for her."

"As do we all. Though, I confess I cannot muster anything but contempt for Lilith's father," Crispin admitted.

"I take it we aren't leaving for Scotland, after all?" Equal parts disappointment and relief shone in Jessica's eyes.

No, the need no longer existed. He shook his head. "There's no reason. There can be no question of Brighton attempting to enforce the betrothal contract now." He smiled, feeling more at ease than he could ever recall. He was free to marry the woman he loved more than life itself. "It's up to you whether you want the banns read or if you'd like to marry by special license."

Jessica's gaze dropped to her hand, and she slowly turned the band around her finger. "I'd rather not wait." Her cheeks pinkened, and when she brought her eyes up to meet his, he knew full well why she didn't want to delay.

By damn, neither did Crispin. Too blasted bad Brentwood hadn't acquired the special license. He'd wed her today, and tonight, he'd introduce her to passion as he showed her and told her in a hundred ways how much he adored her.

The duchess hugged her sister. "I'm happy for you, Jessica. It's obvious to anyone with eyes in their head that you and Bainbridge care deeply for each other." She turned that penetrating stare upon Crispin. "Make my sister happy, Your Grace."

"Indeed, Bainbridge. You must, for if you do not, then *my* lady will not be happy, and that is unacceptable." Sutcliffe extended his hand, and Crispin seized it at once in a firm grip. "Congratulations, my friend."

"Thank you." Crispin drew Jessica to her feet, something which might very well be giddiness cavorting about his middle. "Is three days too long to wait?"

"No." She shook her head, her eyes luminous with love. For him.

Still holding her hand, he turned to Sutcliffe.

He held his hands up, palm outward. "I know. *I know*. You wish to be alone with your intended." Winking, he bent his elbow and held it out for his wife. "I haven't been married so very long that I've forgotten what it was like to be betrothed."

Jessica colored prettily as Crispin drew her into his arms before her sister and brother-in-law made the doorway. The door closed with a soft *snick*, and he buried one hand in her hair and placed the other at the small of her waist, pressing her to him.

He nipped her ear. "I vow, the next three days are going to be the longest of my life, waiting to make you mine."

"Who says we have to wait?" Her voice husky with desire, she peeked at him through her thick lashes.

God help him resist this siren. *Three days.* He had the willpower to resist for three days before he made Jessica his in every way.

"I do, minx." He tweaked her nose.

She stood on her toes and entwined her arms about Crispin's neck. "Well, then I suppose I'll have to persuade you otherwise."

And by God, she almost did.

Almost.

Epilogue

Pickford Hill Park

August 1810

Jessica laughed as she guided her docile black mare, Midnight, around a boulder between the copse of towering oak trees. These past four months had been the happiest of her life. Months of being the Duchess of Bainbridge. Of being Crispin's wife.

At first, she'd been afraid to learn to ride, but as he'd promised she would, she'd taken to the saddle like a duck to water. Pickford Hill Park now boasted eight ducks, four geese, another half dozen hens, two goats, two adorable spaniel puppies—gifts from him—

and a very pregnant barn cat.

No donkey. Yet.

She fully expected to add more animals to her beloved menagerie, but he never complained. He had laughed, quite jubilantly, when she'd insisted on knitting cardigans for the kid goats. A few fervent kisses had shushed him quite effectively. That had led to an interesting bout of lovemaking before the hearth in the drawing room.

What was undoubtedly a dreamy smile curved her mouth. She did rather like that lovemaking business.

"Let's rest here in the shade," Crispin said over his shoulder. The summer's heat yet remained, and their morning ride had left Jessica a trifle overheated.

A small, musical stream meandered along the meadow just beyond the tree stand they'd sought sanctuary within. She just might be persuaded to wade in the chilly depths.

"I've had another letter from Thea," she said as he helped her dismount. He held her against him, permitting her to slide down the length of his sinewy body. When she encountered a familiar swelling, she grinned. She cupped his groin, earning a low growl and a smothered oath. "My, what do we have here?"

"I suppose she's asking us to visit Ridgefield Court again?" He'd buried his face in her neck, muffling his voice. He nuzzled the sensitive spot at the juncture of her throat and shoulder, and it was her turn to moan.

"Yes," she agreed, a trifle distracted when the lump against her hand began to swell. They'd only seen baby Amber twice since her birth. "Nicolette is back from her honeymoon and has promised to spend a week at Ridgewood." Jessica stood on her toes and kissed Crispin's jaw, relishing the faint brush of his clean-shaven skin against her lips.

"I seriously doubted Nicolette would ever marry. And to Westfall, no less." He snorted and shook his head as he tethered the mounts to low-lying branches.

"I know," she laughed and patted Midnight's shiny withers. She'd come to adore the beautiful mare. "And I can scarce believe Rayne and Ophelia have wed, too."

"At this rate, all of my friends will be married

within a year," he muttered, not nearly as disgruntled as he pretended. Married life agreed with him.

And with her.

She met her husband's hungry gaze and gave him a seductive smile. "We've not made love outdoors yet."

His eyebrows dipped low as he slowly scanned the area, his intense gaze coming to rest on the boulder she'd skirted earlier. "Are you suggesting I've been remiss in my husbandly duties, Duchess?"

She giggled then licked her lips. Crispin had always been able to turn her bones to jelly with one look from his quicksilver eyes. "Perhaps just a trifle negligent."

"Then, I must remedy the oversight at once." He stalked toward her, his strapping legs eating up the distance between them, and she retreated, enjoying the chase as much as being captured.

She continued retreating, until she bumped into the dratted boulder, coming up short.

"Oh."

It wasn't large enough to pass for a bed. Scanning

the area, she spied a grassy spot, still relatively secluded by the trees.

Crispin was upon her now, passion already sharpening the angles of his dear face. “Turn around, lady wife.”

“I thought…what?” *Turn around? Whatever for?*

Oh. She complied and wiggled her hips when she felt his hands settle on either side of them. Of a sudden, she was shy, worried they’d be seen. “Crispin, are you sure this is private enough?”

“Quite sure.” Air caressed Jessica’s legs and then her bum as he raised her riding habit. “Trust me, darling. Spread your legs.”

“Always, my love,” she murmured as she complied.

“Let me make up for my negligence, sweetheart,” he breathed into her ear.

“If you insist.” She sighed breathlessly as he slid into her.

And he did. Most satisfactorily.

About the Author

USA Today Bestselling, award-winning author COLLETTE CAMERON® scribbles Scottish and Regency historicals featuring dashing rogues and scoundrels and the intrepid damsels who reform them. Blessed with an overactive and witty muse that won't stop whispering new romantic romps in her ear, she's lived in Oregon her entire life, though she dreams of living in Scotland part-time. A self-confessed Cadbury chocoholic, you'll always find a dash of inspiration and a pinch of humor in her sweet-to-spicy timeless romances®.

Explore **Collette's worlds** at
www.collettecameron.com!

Join her **VIP Reader Club** and **FREE newsletter**.
Giggles guaranteed!

FREE BOOK: Join Collette's The Regency Rose® VIP Reader Club to get updates on book releases, cover reveals, contests and giveaways she reserves exclusively for email and newsletter followers. Also, any deals, sales, or special promotions are offered to club members first. She will not share your name or email, nor will she spam you.

http://bit.ly/TheRegencyRoseGift

Follow Collette on BookBub
https://www.bookbub.com/authors/collette-cameron

Dearest Reader,

Thank you for reading WOOED BY A WICKED DUKE!

I hope you enjoyed a few hours' escape from life's stress and responsibilities and lost yourself in 19th Century Regency England. If you've been reading the other books in my Seductive Scoundrels series, you'll know that Jessica was introduced in A DECEMBER WITH A DUKE.

Jessica is not your typical vicar's daughter, and much like her sister in ONLY A DUKE WOULD DARE, she's secretly been in love with the book's hero. Only Crispin, the Duke of Bainbridge, has a wicked, wicked reputation. No self-respecting clergyman's daughter would ever acknowledge a *tendre* for such a man.

Despite his roguish history, Crispin is a gentleman. Betrothed since he was a child, he won't act upon his hidden feelings for Jessica. However, fate took matters into her own hands, and the results lead to a scandal but an unexpected chance at love as well.

If you enjoy reading friends to lovers, duke, arranged marriage, or class difference love stories with a pinch of mystery, a dash of humor, and gripping emotion, then you'll adore my enthralling

SEDUCTIVE SCOUNDRELS SERES. Settle into your favorite reading nook for page-turning, entertaining Regency world adventures you can't put down.

You can read the first chapter of all of my books on my website and on Facebook. Please consider telling other readers why you enjoyed this book by reviewing it. I truly adore hearing from my readers. You can contact me at my website below. I also have a fabulous VIP Reader Group on Facebook. If you're a fan of my books and historical romance, I'd love to have you join me. That link is below as well.

Please consider telling other readers why you enjoyed this book by reviewing it. I adore hearing from my readers.

Here's wishing you many happy hours of reading, more happily-ever-afters than you can possibly enjoy in a lifetime, and abundant blessings to you and your loved ones.

Collette Cameron

What Would a Duke Do?

Seductive Scoundrels Book Four
A Historical Regency Romance

He's bent on revenge. She's his enemy's granddaughter. He'll marry her...willing or not.

Maxwell, the Duke of Pennington, is a man focused on one thing: revenge. He'll stop at nothing to achieve his goal, including marrying the beautiful, unpredictable granddaughter of the man he seeks reprisal against—whether Gabriella is willing or not. As Max inexplicably finds himself drawn to the spirited minx, unforeseen doubts and guilt arise.

Miss Gabriella Breckensole is astonished when the enigmatic Duke of Pennington turns his romantic attentions on her. Debonair and confident, he set her heart fluttering from their first meeting. Far beneath his station, Gabby never hoped to win his favor, and she soon risks losing her heart to the roguish lord.

Until she accidentally overhears Maxwell vowing to return her familial home to his dukedom and learns his courtship is a revenge-filled ploy. Even though he awakened feelings she never imagined possible, Gabriella now considers him an enemy. Can Max make the impossible choice between retribution or forever losing the only woman to ever touch his heart?

What Would a Duke Do?

Seductive Scoundrels, Book Four

December 1809

Ridgewood Court, Essex England

Humming beneath her breath, Gabriella Breckensole practically skipped down the stairs on her way to meet the other female houseguests to make kissing boughs and other festive decorations. The past few days had been a whirlwind of activity, as her hostess, Theadosia, the Duchess of Sutcliffe and one of her dearest friends, hosted a Christmastide house party, the likes of which Essex had never witnessed before.

The event was made all that much more enjoyable by the presence of Maxwell Woolbright, the Duke of Pennington. Since Gabriella and her twin sister had returned from finishing school almost two years ago, she'd encountered him at a few gatherings. He was quite the most dashing man she'd ever met, and despite being far above her station, she thrilled whenever he directed his attention her way.

Descending the last riser, she puzzled for a moment. Where were the ladies to meet? The drawing room, the floral salon, or the dining room? Forehead scrunched, she pulled her mouth to the side and started toward the drawing room. Halfway there, she remembered they were to meet in the slightly larger dining room. She spun around and marched the other direction, passing the impressive library, its door slightly ajar.

"Harold Breckensole will pay for what he's done," a man declared in an angry, gruff voice.

Gabriella halted mid-step, her stomach plunging to

her slippered feet. She swiftly looked up and down the vacant corridor before tiptoeing to the cracked doorway. Who spoke about her grandfather with such hostility?

Breath held, she peeked through the narrow opening. The Dukes of Sutcliffe, Pennington, and Sheffield stood beside the fireplace, facing each other.

Pennington held a glass of umber-colored spirits in one hand as he stared morosely into the capering flames. “I shall reclaim Hartfordshire Court. I swear.”

“You say the estate was once part of the unentailed part of the duchy?” Sutcliffe asked, concern forming a line between his eyebrows.

Pennington tossed back a swallow of his drink. “Yes. It belonged to my grandmother’s family for generations, and after what I’ve recently learned, I mean to see it restored to the ducal holdings, come hell or high water. And I’ll destroy Breckensole too.”

Slapping a hand over her mouth, she backed away, shaking her head as stinging tears slid from the corners of her eyes.

Oh my God. She’d been halfway to falling in love

with a man bent on revenge of some sort. Gabriella jutted her chin up, angrily swiping at her cheeks. The Duke of Pennington had just become her enemy.

1

Late March 1810

Colechester, Essex, England

"Miss Breckensole, what an unexpected…pleasure," a man drawled in a cultured voice, the merest hint of laughter coloring his melodious baritone.

Unexpected and wholly unwelcome.

Gabriella froze in her admiration of Nicolette Twistleton's adorable pug puppy and barely refrained from gnashing her teeth. She knew full well who stood behind her. The odious, arrogant—*annoying as*

Hades—Maxwell, Duke of Pennington. His delicious cologne wafted past her nostrils, and she let her eyelids drift half shut as she ordered her heart to resume its regular cadence.

He didn't know what she'd discovered about him. That he was a dishonorable, deceiving blackguard behind his oh-so-charming demeanor. And he meant to destroy her grandfather. That knowledge bolstered her courage and settled her erratic pulse.

One midnight eyebrow arched questioningly, Nicolette threw her a harried glance before dipping into a curtsy. "Your Grace."

Gabriella hadn't confided in Nicolette. Hadn't confided in anyone as to why she disliked him so very much. Quashing her irritation at his appearance and his daring to greet her as if they were the greatest of friends, she schooled her features into blandness before turning and sinking into the expected deferential greeting. "Duke."

He bowed, his strong mouth slanted into his usual half-mocking smile. "What brings you to town?" He glanced around. "Your sister or grandmother aren't with you? Or an abigail, either?" A hint of disapproval edged his observation. "Did you come with Miss Twistleton?"

Beast. Who was he to question her conduct? She wasn't accountable to him.

"No, I am here with my mother." Nicolette cast Gabriella another bewildered glance. "She's at the milliner's."

Surely he was aware, as was the whole of Colechester, that a lady's maid was an unnecessary expense, according to Gabriella's grandfather. That the duke so offhandedly and publicly made mention of the deficiency angered and chagrined her.

Pennington turned an expectant look upon her. As if he were entitled to have an answer because, after all, *he* was the much sought-after Duke of Pennington.

Edging her chin upward, Gabriella clutched her packages tighter, one of which was her twin's birthday present. She saved for months to be able to surprise Ophelia with the mazarine-blue velvet cloak.

"Grandmama is unwell, and Ophelia stayed home to care for her." She wouldn't offer him further explanation.

"I am truly sorry to hear that. May I have my physician call upon her?" he asked, all solicitousness, even going so far as to lower his brows as if he truly cared. A concern she knew to be feigned, given what she'd overheard at the Duke and Duchess of Sutcliffe's Christmastide house party last December.

"That's not necessary. She was seen by one only last week." My, she sounded positively unaffected. The epitome of a self-possessed, gently-bred young woman.

Inside, she fumed at his forwardness.

How she wanted to rail at him. To tell him precisely what she thought of his nefarious scheme. Why did he—*conceited, handsome rakehell*—have to be in Colechester today too? He promptly turned her much-anticipated afternoon outing sour. Freshly cut lemon or gooseberry face-puckering, attitude-ruining sour.

And why he insisted upon trying to speak to her at every opportunity, she couldn't conceive. Three months ago, and on the few unfortunate occasions they'd come across each other since she'd made her feelings perfectly clear—to-the-point-of-rudeness-clear.

She'd heard him vow to the Dukes of Sheffield and Sutcliffe that, "*come hell or high water*"—Pennington's very sternly muttered words—he'd reclaim the lands that had once been an unentailed part of the duchy. Lands that had belonged to his grandmother's family for generations.

Property, which included her beloved home, Hartfordshire Court. A holding that Grandpapa had purchased, fair and square, from the duke's own degenerate grandfather decades before and which, with hard work and industry, he had made prosperous.

"Mama is so very pleased you are to attend our musical assembly, Your Grace," Nicolette blurted. As if sensing the stilted silence and not understanding the reason why but wanting to defuse the tangible awkwardness.

Unable to contain her disbelief, Gabriella sent him a quick glance from beneath her lashes. *He is to attend? Of all the dashed rotten luck.* He rarely remained at his country seat past mid-March. London held far more appeal to a man of the world like him, and truth be told, she had anticipated—*needed*—a few months' reprieve from his presence.

She and Ophelia were to attend as well, but now she no longer anticipated her first social foray, other than tea these past two months, as she had but a minute ago.

Nicolette shifted the puppy and received a wet tongue on the cheek for her efforts. "No licking, Bella," she admonished whilst rubbing the pup behind her ears. "It's also Gabriella's birthday that day," she offered with an impish twinkle in her eye. "She'll be one and twenty."

Gabriella shot her a quelling glance. The world—*he*—didn't need to know she was practically on the shelf with no prospects save spinsterhood.

"I quite look forward to the entertainment." Insincerity rang in his tone as he gave a gracious nod and continued staring at Gabriella. "And, also, to wish you a happy day, Miss Breckensole." The latter held a note of authenticity. He flicked his gaze down the street, seeming uncharacteristically uncertain. “Ladies, would you join me for a cup of chocolate or coffee?”

The Prince’s Coffee House was but four doors down and was acclaimed not only for its hot beverages but the ambiance and scrumptious pastries. Not that Gabriella had ever sampled either.

She’d wanted to, but Grandpapa frowned upon eating in the village. A waste of good coin, he grumbled.

Nicolette shook her head, no genuine regret shadowing her face. After being jilted, she bore disdain for every male, save her brother, the Earl of Scarborough. “I fear Mama is expecting me inside. I only came outside for Bella’s sake.”

“And I must return home straightaway.” Gabriella signaled her driver with a flick of her wrist and slant of her head. She’d finished her shopping before bumping into Nicolette and the newest addition to the Twistleton household.

Amid a chorus of creaks and groans, her grandfather’s slightly lopsided and dated coach pulled alongside her. Jackson, the groomsman, climbed down and, after three rigorous attempts, managed to lower the steps. She passed him her parcels, which he promptly placed inside the conveyance.

"Please allow me." The duke stepped forward and offered his hand to assist her inside.

While she wanted to give him the cut by refusing to accept his offer, Nicolette was sure to interrogate her as to why she'd been so rude the next time they met. A year ago, even three months ago, Gabriella would've been overjoyed at his attention. Now, he was her enemy. A handsome, dangerous, cunning, and unpredictable nemesis.

As lightly as she was able, she placed her fingertips atop his palm and entered the rickety, out-of-fashion, forty-year-old coach. Lips melded, she studiously disregarded the alarming jolt of sensation zipping up her arm at his touch. She should feel nothing but contempt for him and most assuredly entertain no carnal attraction.

The duke didn't immediately close the door behind her. His gaze probed hers for a long sliver of a moment, and suddenly the coach became very confining. And hot. She waved her hand before her face, having left her fan at home. "Might I call upon you tomorrow?" *Is he utterly daft?* "Perhaps we might take a ride? Naturally, Miss Ophelia is welcome too."

That latter seemed more of an afterthought. He knew she couldn't ride out alone with him, and he was mad as a Bedlam guest if he truly believed she'd willingly spend time in his company.

Gabriella met his gaze straight on. Something undefinable shadowed the depths of his unusual eyes—one green and one blue. "I must decline, Your Grace. I also must ask you, once again, to direct your attention elsewhere. I am not now, nor will I ever be, receptive to them."

If she never spoke to him again, it would be too soon.

Did he really think just because he was a duke and she was the lowly granddaughter of a gentleman-farmer, she'd jump at the opportunity to spend time in his company?

You did at one time. And suffered a broken heart when his true character became evident.

Not. Anymore. Never again. Not when she knew his true motivation for seeking her company. How much her feelings had changed for him these past months.

At once, his striking countenance grew shuttered, his high cheekbones more pronounced with…anger? Disappointment? “We, shall see, *chérie*. We shall see.”

“What, precisely, do you mean by that?” Something very near dread clogged her throat, and the words came out husky rather than terse as she’d intended.

Instead of answering, he offered an enigmatic smile and doffed his hat, the afternoon sunlight glinting on his raven hair. “Good day.”

We shall see, chérie. We shall see. His words replaying over and over in her mind, she remained immobile, her focus trained on his retreating form until he disappeared into the Pony and Pint instead of The Prince’s Coffee House. At one time, she’d fancied herself enamored of him. She’d been flattered he’d turned his ducal attention on her: a simple country girl without prospects.

Firmly stifling those memories and the associated emotions, she tapped the roof. "Home. Jackson, and do hurry. Grandmama needs her medicines."

And I need to put distance between myself and the Duke of Pennington. Because even though she knew the truth, a tiny part of her heart yet ached for him, and she loathed herself for that weakness.

Two hours later, shivering and briskly rubbing her arms, Gabriella bent forward to peer out the coach window again.

Tentatively probing her head, she winced. The knot from smacking her noggin on the side of the vehicle when the axle snapped hadn't grown any larger. Neither did it bleed. Nonetheless, the walnut-sized lump ached with the ferocity of a newly trapped tiger. A superbly large, sharp-toothed, and foul-tempered beast.

"Really," she muttered, exasperated and uncharacteristically cross from hunger, cold, and the painful bump. "Whatever can be taking Jackson so long to return? Hartsfordshire Court isn't so very blasted far."

Less than two miles, she estimated after another glance at the familiar green meadow sloping to the winding river beyond. The recent rains caused the brown-tinged water to run high and spill over its banks, as it did nearly every spring. In the summer, the lush grasslands fed Grandpapa's famed South Devon cattle on one side and their neighbor, the Duke of Pennington's, fluffy, black-faced sheep on the other.

An uncharitable thought about the distinction between the keen intelligence of cows and sheep's lack of acumen tried to form, but she squelched it. It wasn't the poor sheep's fault she couldn't abide their owner.

After repeatedly assuring her hesitant coachman she would be perfectly fine until he returned with the seldom-used phaeton, Jackson had swiftly stridden away. Not, however, without turning to work his worried gaze over her, the team, and the disabled coach's crippled wheel thrice. Each time, she donned a smile wide enough to crack her cheeks and made a shooing motion for him to continue.

For pity's sake. She wasn't one of those silly, simpering misses afraid the hem of her skirt might become dusty or who shrieked hysterically upon a cobweb brushing her gloves or cheek. So long as the resident eight-fuzzy-legged spider had *long* since removed itself to a new home.

If it weren't for her impractical footwear, Gabriella would've walked as well. But she'd no wish for bruised feet or the lecture certain to follow from dear Grandpapa about the cost of replacing ruined slippers. And that would probably produce another discourse about unnecessary trips to Colechester for what he deemed nonsensical fripperies.

Perhaps they were absurd to a man given to wearing the same staid suit and shoes for the past five years as Grandpapa had been. But Ophelia's birthday present wasn't a silly frippery. Neither was Grandmama's medicine nor the chemises for Gabriella and her sister frivolous expenses. It had been three years since anyone had purchased new undergarments.

With her leftover pin money—one half crown

every month—Gabriella had purchased the beloved hunch-shouldered curmudgeon his favorite blend of pipe tobacco. Oh, he'd grumble and grouse over the wasteful spending, but she hadn't a doubt she'd earn a kiss upon her forehead before he shuffled off to enjoy a pipe and a tot in his fusty study amongst his even fustier tomes.

A wry smile quirked her mouth.

Did Grandpapa use the same tobacco five times as he insisted Grandmama do with tea leaves? Anything to save a penny or two. The Breckensoles didn't enjoy neat lumps of white sugar in their tea, either but rather the golden-brown nubs chiseled from a cheaper, hard-as-a-blasted-boulder loaf. Since they never—truly never—had guests for tea, or for any other occasion for that matter, there was no need to feel a trifle embarrassed at the economy.

She ran a gloved finger over the lumpy parcel containing the umber-brown bottles for her grandmother. A month ago, a nasty cough had settled in Grandmama's lungs, and she couldn't shake the ailment.

Gabriella's current discomfort tugged her meandering musings back to her immediate situation. For all of two seconds—fine, mayhap three—she'd considered riding home atop one of the horses still harnessed to the coach. But that would've required hiking her gown knee-high and riding astride. Even she daren't that degree of boldness.

Nonetheless, on days she yearned to toss aside society's and her strict grandparents' constraints, she *might've* been known to sneak a horse from the stables and ride along the river, bonnet-free and skirts rucked most inappropriately high. Oh, the freedom was wondrous, though the tell-tale freckles that were wont to sprout upon her nose usually gave her recklessness away.

Her grandparents never lectured, but their silent disapproval was sufficient to quell her hoydenish ways. For a week or two.

The carriage made an eerie noise, the way a vehicle sounded in the throes of death. *If* a vehicle were capable of such a thing. Another juddering crack followed as the damaged side wedged deeper into the dirt.

She let loose a softly sworn oath no respectable woman ought to know, let alone utter aloud, as she grabbed the seat to keep from tumbling onto the floor. A labored groan and a piercing creak followed on the heels of her crude vulgarity, and a five-inch-long jagged crack split the near window.

"Blast and damn."

A new chill skidded down her spine as she mentally braced herself for Grandpapa's intense displeasure. He'd be aggravated about the damage to the coach, but more so about the cost to repair it. A frugal, self-made man, he was as reluctant to part with a coin as he was to leave Hartfordshire Court. Others who didn't know him well called him stingy and miserly.

In the fifteen years since coming to live at Hartfordshire, Gabriella could count on two hands the number of times either grandparent had left the estate. She would shrivel up and die if forced to stay there months on end.

Yet her hermit-like grandparents had been diligent

in assuring she and her sister never lacked for company or social interactions. They'd even conceded to send the twins to finishing school. At no little cost, either. What a juxtaposition. Her grandparents eschewed all things social, but she and her sister craved the routs, soirees, balls, picnics, musical parties, and all else that guaranteed a superior assemblage.

One troublesome, unignorable fact remained unaddressed, however: Grandpapa had never spoken of a dowry for either of them. They'd never wanted for necessities, but Gabriella suspected his pockets weren't as flush as he'd have his family believe.

Her heart gave a queer pang. It wasn't exactly worry or distress. But neither was the peculiar feeling of frustration or disappointment. Nevertheless, it left her unsettled. Discontent and restless. Disconcerted about what her future might entail. Ophelia's too.

As improbable as it was, except for splurging on the matched team and phaeton, her grandfather had been noticeably less inclined to spend money after the twins returned home two years ago. Now, at almost one and twenty, with their aging grandparents' health beginning to fail and their neighbor, the mercenary Duke of Pennington, bent on stealing Hartsfordshire Court from them, Gabriella fretted about what would happen to her sister if neither of them married soon.

There weren't exactly men, noble or otherwise, scurrying to form a queue to court either of them. Or to dance with them at assemblies or request romantic strolls through opulent gardens. No posies, sweets, or poems found their way to the house's front door on a regular basis, either. On *any* basis, for that matter.

Oh, the country gentlemen were kind and polite enough. Indeed, some aristocrats and gentry, even a rogue or two, had been downright charming and flirtatious. More than one had hinted they'd very much like to pursue an immoral liaison. But the simple truth was as obvious as a giraffe's purple tongue sampling pea soup in the dining room: Dowerless, Gabriella's and Ophelia's prospects were few.

Nonexistent, truth to tell.

For one horrid, ugly fact couldn't be overlooked: a woman without a dowry, no matter how refined, immaculately fitted out, or proficient in French, Latin,

Spanish, painting, playing the pianoforte—or the violin in Gabriella's case—and managing a household she might be, without the lure of a marriage settlement to entice a respectable suitor, such an unfortunate lady was labeled an undesirable.

And much like other hapless women in the same ill-fated predicament, spinsterhood, dark and foreboding, loomed on the horizon, a slightly terrifying fate for any young woman.

Which made the duke's interest in her all the more questionable. He couldn't possibly have honorable intentions.

She pursed her mouth, drawing her eyebrows into a taut line. Barbaric, this business of bribing a man with money, land, and the good Lord only knew what else to take a woman to wife. Why couldn't love be enough?

Like Theadosia and Sutcliffe? Or her maternal cousin Everleigh and the Duke of Sheffield? Or even Jemmah and Jules, the Duke and Duchess of Dandridge? Once, not so long ago, Gabriella had yearned for that kind of love. Had dared to hope she might've found it, but the object of her affections had turned out to be a colossal rat.

Unfortunately, such was the nature of the Marriage Mart. Without dowries, Gabriella and her twin could look forward to caring for their grandparents into their dotage rather than marry and have families. Their lack of suitors could be laid at Society's silk-clad feet. Strictures, along with a goodly portion of greed and hunger for power, dictated most matches. That, regrettably, was an indisputable fact.

Something uncomfortable and slightly terrifying, much like melancholy, turned over in her breast and swirled in her stomach. To distract herself from her somber reflections, she inspected the lonely road once more.

The fading afternoon sun filtering through the towering evergreen treetops on the other side of the deserted track confirmed dusk's dark cloak and chill would blanket the countryside soon. For at least the sixth time in the past hour, Gabriella examined the dainty timepiece pinned to her spencer.

She frowned and gave it a little shake. Was the

deuced thing working?

Yes, the big hand shifted just then. She huffed out a small, petulant sigh, for she recognized her own impatience.

Where the devil was Jackson, for pity's sake? Had something waylaid him? *Obviously.* Yes, but what? The unbidden thoughts agitated her already-heightened nerves. Nerves that had been fraught since departing the village earlier.

Angered anew at Pennington's audacity, she pressed her lips into an irritated line and fisted her hands. Only he had the ability to make her so peeved. *Bloody, greedy bounder. By Jove, didn't he have enough? Why must he covet what we have, too?*

Chartworth Hall was an immense estate boasting some two thousand acres, a mansion—more castle than house—a hunting lodge, a dower house, embarrassingly massive and full stables, and numerous other outbuildings.

Why the duke focused on Hartfordshire's acres and seventeen-room residence, quite desperately in need of refurbishing and restoration, made no sense at all. She didn't know the particulars of the sale. Neither did she understand how the unentailed property came to be adjacent to the entailed lands, but she didn't give a fig.

What she *did* care about was the duke's callousness. His insensitivity and cold-heartedness. He hadn't a thought for any of the Breckensoles, of displacing them from their home. Oh, no. His only concern was how to cheat Grandpapa out of his property and to expand the already enormous ducal holdings.

By God, she wouldn't permit it. She would not.

A Diamond for a Duke

Seductive Scoundrels Series Book One
A Historical Regency Romance

A dour duke. A wistful wallflower. An impossible match.

Jules, Sixth Duke of Dandridge, disdains Society and all its trappings, preferring the country's solitude and peace. Already jaded after the woman he loved died years ago, he's become even more so since unexpectedly inheriting a dukedom's responsibilities and finding himself the target of every husband-hunting vixen and matchmaker mother in London.

Jemmah Dament has adored Jules from afar for years—since before her family's financial and social reversals. She dares not dream she can win a duke's heart any more than she hopes to escape the life of servitude imposed on her by an uncaring mother. Jemmah knows full well Jules is too far above her station now. Besides, his family has already selected his perfect duchess: a poised, polished, exquisite blueblood.

A chance encounter reunites Jules and Jemmah, resulting in a passionate interlude neither can forget. Jules realizes he wants more—much more—than Jemmah's sweet kisses or her warming his bed. He must somehow convince her to gamble on a dour duke. But can Jemmah trust a man promised to another? One who's sworn never to love again?

Only a Duke Would Dare

Seductive Scoundrels Series Book Two
A Historical Regency Romance

"Delightful, dazzling, and oh-so-delicious." ~Cheryl Bolen,* NYT *Bestselling Author

A reluctant duke. A vicar's daughter. A forbidden love.

Marriage—an unpleasant obligation

A troublesome addendum to his father's will requires Victor, Duke of Sutcliffe, to marry before his twenty-seventh birthday or lose his fortune. After a three-year absence, he ventures home, intent upon finding the most biddable and forgettable miss in Essex. A woman who will make no demands upon him and won't mind being left behind when he returns to London. Except, Victor meets Theadosia Brentwood again and finds himself powerless to resist her—even if she is promised to another and the exact opposite of what he thought he wanted in a duchess.

Marriage—an impossible choice

Secretly in love with Victor for years, Theadosia is overjoyed when he returns. Until she learns he must marry within mere weeks. When he unexpectedly proposes, she must make an impossible decision. How can Thea elope with him when he's marrying out of necessity, not love? Besides, if she does wed Victor, her betrothed—a man she loathes—will reveal a scandalous secret. A secret that will send her father to prison and leave her sister and mother homeless.

A December with a Duke

Seductive Scoundrels Book Three
A Historical Regency Romance

He's entirely the wrong sort of man. That's what makes him so utterly *right.*

After a horrific marriage, widow Everleigh Chatterton is cynical and leery of men. She rarely ventures into society, and when she must, she barely speaks to them. As a favor to a friend, she reluctantly agrees to attend a Christmas house party. Unfortunately, Griffin, Duke of Sheffield, is also in attendance. Even though Everleigh has previously snubbed him, she can't deny her attraction to the confident, darkly handsome duke.

For almost a year, Griffin has searched for the perfect duchess to help care for the orphan he's taken on. He sets his sights on the exquisite-but-unapproachable Everleigh Chatterton after her sweet interactions with the child impress him. He is convinced he can thaw her icy exterior and free the warm, passionate woman lurking behind the arctic facade. Only, as Griffin pursues her, it's his heart that's transformed.

Can Everleigh learn to trust and love again? Will Griffin get his Christmas wish and make her his bride? Or has he underestimated her wounds and fears and be forced to let her go?

Printed in Great Britain
by Amazon

56409842R00163